"What were we doing in the summer when we were sixteen?"

His eyes seemed to drink her in, and Sienna blushed, uncertain where the conversation was headed.

"Getting pizza, riding horses, hopping on four-wheelers, going to the rodeo and any other local attraction that pulled into town." She had fond memories of those days. They'd been the most carefree ones she'd ever experienced.

"Then we should make sure Connor and Lily have the same thing."

There he went again, using the word *we*.

"I appreciate what you're saying, Blaine, but I've imposed too much already." She didn't want him to think she was ungrateful, but Connor and Lily were her responsibility, not his. "We don't have to do anything. I thought it was important for you to know what's going on. That's it."

She couldn't have asked for a better response from Blaine, but it was dangerous accepting his help. Sixteen was a lifetime ago, and reliving it with Blaine, Lily and Connor might make her want more. She'd been blessed to enjoy it once. Happiness like that didn't come around twice.

Jill Kemerer writes novels with love, humor and faith. Besides spoiling her mini dachshund and keeping up with her busy kids, Jill reads stacks of books, lives for her morning coffee and gushes over fluffy animals. She resides in Ohio with her husband and two children. Jill loves connecting with readers, so please visit her website, jillkemerer.com, or contact her at PO Box 2802, Whitehouse, OH 43571.

Books by Jill Kemerer

Love Inspired

Wyoming Ranchers

The Prodigal's Holiday Hope
A Cowboy to Rely On
Guarding His Secret
The Mistletoe Favor
Depending on the Cowboy

Wyoming Sweethearts

Her Cowboy Till Christmas
The Cowboy's Secret
The Cowboy's Christmas Blessings
Hers for the Summer

Wyoming Cowboys

The Rancher's Mistletoe Bride
Reunited with the Bull Rider
Wyoming Christmas Quadruplets
His Wyoming Baby Blessing

Visit the Author Profile page at LoveInspired.com for more titles.

Depending on the Cowboy

Jill Kemerer

LOVE INSPIRED
INSPIRATIONAL ROMANCE

LOVE INSPIRED®
INSPIRATIONAL ROMANCE

Recycling programs
for this product may
not exist in your area.

ISBN-13: 978-1-335-58550-9

Depending on the Cowboy

Copyright © 2023 by Ripple Effect Press, LLC

For questions and comments about the quality of this book, please contact us
at CustomerService@Harlequin.com.

Love Inspired
22 Adelaide St. West, 41st Floor
Toronto, Ontario M5H 4E3, Canada
www.LoveInspired.com

Printed in U.S.A.

Remember ye not the former things,
neither consider the things of old. Behold,
I will do a new thing; now it shall spring forth;
shall ye not know it? I will even make a way
in the wilderness, and rivers in the desert.
—*Isaiah* 43:18–19

To my good friend Kristina Knight, whom I can always count on to ooh and aah over texts of puppies and baby goats. Love you, Kristi!

Chapter One

Women made him nervous. Pregnant women? Well, they terrified him.

Blaine Mayer gave the kitchen counter one last swipe, then straightened the pillows on the couch in the three-bedroom log cabin down the lane from his ranch house. The former foreman's home had been collecting dust for over a year. And that wouldn't do for when Sienna arrived.

Sienna Norden—Sienna Powell now. Blaine had good memories of being her lab partner in high school biology and hanging out with her and their friends on the weekends until she moved to Casper, Wyoming, right before junior year. She'd been one of the only women he'd ever considered easy to talk to, aside from his sisters, and they didn't count.

It had been jarring last fall when his sister Erica, now married and living in Casper, had announced she'd run in to Sienna. Since then, the two women had become good friends. When Mom had informed him a week ago that Sienna—pregnant and recently divorced—was bringing her niece and nephew to Mayer Canyon Ranch for the next two months, Blaine hadn't put up a fight.

It wasn't like he had a say in it, anyhow. Erica, too, was having a baby, and Blaine knew better than to argue with her. It would only cause tears or a battle. No thank you. Honestly, he didn't mind Sienna and her crew staying here for most of the summer. It had been lonelier than he'd expected when he'd moved to his half of the sprawling family ranch in Sunrise Bend, Wyoming, last year.

He gave the place a quick once-over. Yep, the cabin was ready. All morning he and his mother had disinfected and deodorized it. Mom had brought over new bedspreads for the guest rooms, and she'd made sure there were plenty of fluffy towels. To say she was tickled pink to be getting Sienna as a part-time helper for the candle shop *and* two teens to spoil for all of June and July would be the understatement of the century.

Blaine just hoped having them a mere hop, skip and jump away wouldn't affect his plans for the ranch. He'd been riding out every afternoon to what he and Jet, his big brother and owner of the other half of the ranch, jokingly referred to as the dead pasture on Grandpa's land—Blaine's land now.

Blaine was convinced it could be a good source of additional hay. Last fall, he'd killed the weeds. This spring, he'd reseeded the entire pasture with drought-resistant wheatgrass.

It had been expensive. And risky.

With the dry conditions this year, he might have been better off keeping the pasture free for the cattle to graze. Now that it had been reseeded, it couldn't be grazed for two entire growing seasons. Jet, naturally, thought he was making a mistake and had told him so on more than one occasion. Maybe his brother was right.

What if the cattle ran out of grazing land this winter? What if the pasture didn't produce the hay he anticipated?

How would he feed his herd?

His phone rang, and he reluctantly took the call, stepping onto the front porch and closing the door behind him. "Blaine speaking."

"Oh, good." A woman with a no-nonsense voice sighed. "I'm glad I caught you. It's Laura Cane. Ralph's daughter."

"Hi, Laura." Blaine had spent plenty of time on the Canes' farm as a teen. Ralph was an expert at breeding and training Australian shepherds as working dogs. Ten years ago, the man had moved an hour south to spend more time with his daughter. Blaine missed helping out with all those dog litters. "How's your dad doing?"

She hesitated, and he got a funny feeling he was about to hear bad news. "Actually, that's why I'm calling. Dad passed away two days ago. Frank and I are planning the funeral, and I don't know how to ask this, but... well, Tiara is due to have her pups within the week. I can't take off work to raise the puppies, and Dad would want Tiara and Ollie to go to someone with experience. You're the only one I could think of who could raise her pups. Dad promised two locals first dibs, so you'd have to find homes for the others if she has more. I know it's a lot to ask."

"I'm sorry about your dad." Blaine swallowed the regret that was lodged in his throat. He wished he had taken the time to drive down there and visit Ralph. Had thought about it several times over the past couple of years, but he'd never acted on it. And now, it was too late. "I didn't realize he was having health problems."

"He died in his sleep. It was unexpected, but he was eighty-two. We were blessed to have him as long as we did. The funeral's the day after tomorrow. I can text you the details if you'd like."

"Would you? My folks will want to come, too." Blaine figured she had a lot of arrangements to make, so he'd better get back to the reason for her call. He descended the porch steps and headed toward the gravel drive. "I take it both dogs are Australian shepherds...?" Blaine couldn't imagine Ralph breeding any other kind.

"Yes, Tiara is Lady Di's grandpup. Dad bought Ollie three years ago from a breeder in Montana. Beautiful dog. Those two are like an old married couple. I won't separate them, and they're too special to stop breeding. Would you be willing to consider adopting them both?"

He'd been there when Lady Di had her final litter. "I'll take Tiara and Ollie for now and raise this litter, but I'm going to have to think about continuing to breed them. It's a big commitment. Why don't I give you a call in a few months after the puppies are weaned? We can figure out where to go from there."

"I was hoping you'd say that. Thank you, Blaine. I'll bring them over this afternoon."

This afternoon? He opened his mouth to speak, but she'd already hung up. He pocketed the phone, his mind reeling with everything he'd need to do to prepare for a pregnant dog due any minute.

The rumble of tires alerted him that Sienna had arrived. Hopefully, her niece and nephew liked dogs, because he was going to need a lot of help when Tiara had her pups.

The silver crossover SUV came to a stop near where Blaine was standing. Both front doors opened, and one of the back doors, too. A tall, lanky teen unfolded his legs from the passenger seat. He had shaggy, dark brown hair, and he was wearing loose-fitting jeans, a black T-shirt and athletic shoes. The girl from the back seat stretched her arms over her head and smiled. Her hazel eyes widened and sparkled as she looked around. She had on light gray jogging pants and a pink T-shirt that said Be Happy. Long, unruly light brown hair trailed down her back.

Sienna stepped out of the driver's seat, letting out an *oof* as she placed a hand on her round belly.

Blaine inhaled sharply. She was still a stunner. Her wavy, dark red hair was a few inches shorter than he remembered, but he noticed her dimples hadn't changed a bit as she tossed him a smile. Took him right back to fifteen, stuttering pulse and all.

Enough of that. This was a platonic arrangement. Nothing more.

"Hope you had a good trip." He tipped his cowboy hat to her in greeting.

"It was good. Uneventful." Sienna slowly walked his way.

He braced himself. Should he hug her? Thrust out his hand? Back up and nod?

The decision was made for him as she held out her arms. He gave her an awkward hug with two quick pats on the back. Flames of embarrassment licked his neck, and he was pretty sure his face resembled a tomato.

"This is my nephew, Connor, and my niece, Lily." Sienna stretched out her arm to indicate the two teens and angled her neck to the side as they approached. They both said hi. "We're all excited to spend the summer here. It was kind of you to offer to put us up."

Well, technically Erica had offered, and Mom had been the one to volunteer his cabin for the three of them since it was the largest guesthouse on either side of the ranch. But Sienna didn't need to know all that.

"Glad to have you," Blaine said. "Want to tour the cabin before unloading?"

"Sure." Sienna beamed as she put her arm around Lily's shoulders and ambled toward the porch. Connor followed behind them, looking like he felt out of place. Blaine knew the feeling well. He'd spent a good portion of his life trailing two steps behind everyone else, especially his big brother.

He loped ahead and held open the front door for the trio, and when they were inside, he pointed out the bedrooms, bathroom and the large mudroom/laundry room off the kitchen.

"Wow, Aunt Sienna, this is amazing." Lily spun in a circle in the living room, looking up at the vaulted ceilings. "It's like a mountain getaway."

"Without the mountains," Blaine added cheerfully. "At least you can see them in the distance."

"Isn't this great, Connor?" Lily asked.

"Yeah, it is, Lil." His expression was hard to read, but his tone was pleasant enough.

The kids disappeared to claim their bedrooms, leaving Blaine and Sienna alone. His tongue must have tied itself into a knot, because he had no idea what to say.

"I really appreciate this, Blaine." Her big green eyes looked suspiciously watery. His gut clenched. The last time Erica was home, he'd asked her how she was doing, and she'd burst into tears and then jogged to the bathroom to throw up.

He was not making that mistake again.

"It's no problem," he said. "I lived in this cabin last year for a few months while I remodeled Grandpa's place. If you need me for anything, I'm in the big house down the lane."

"I saw it." She nodded. "You've done well for yourself. I figured this was what you'd be doing. Ranching always fit you like a glove."

She thought he'd done well for himself? Pride rushed through him, only to be dampened. Blaine was still feeling his way on making big decisions.

Their father had always been in charge until Blaine's youngest brother, Cody, had died a few years ago. Jet had taken over their father's duties while the man grieved. Then Dad retired, insisting Jet and Blaine divide the ranch between them, since their sisters weren't interested in raising cattle. The past year of being his own boss had been an eye-opener. And stressful.

"I hear you're still living in Casper," Blaine said.

"I am. I work for the community college. I'm the coordinator for special projects compliance. Basically, I help find and oversee grants. I'm thankful to have the summer off." A cloud crossed her face. "I needed this summer off."

"Yeah, I can see… Um, congratulations…" He gestured toward her baby bump.

"Thanks." Her dimples flashed again as she cradled her stomach. "I'm due in late August. Your sister helped me through a tough time. I can't wait until she has her baby, too."

"Yeah, uh…" He rubbed the back of his neck. All this

pregnancy talk had him way out of his element. "Why don't I go get your luggage?" Before waiting for her reply, he pivoted and strode out the front door.

Idiot. This was Sienna, not some stranger. He couldn't even hold a conversation for two minutes? No wonder he was single.

Not that he wanted to change his status.

He marched to the back of the SUV, opened the hatch and started grabbing suitcases.

Connor jogged up next to him. "Here, I'll help."

"Okay." Blaine gave the kid a brief glance. "I'm assuming your aunt wants all this inside, so take whatever you can carry."

Connor hefted a large bin into his arms before falling in step next to Blaine. "Aunt Sienna said Lily and I will be helping out around here."

Blaine's mom had mentioned Sienna working part-time at the candle shop, but she hadn't said what Lily and Connor would be doing. Hopefully, enjoying their summer vacation.

"Can I help around the ranch? I don't want to hurt my aunt's feelings, but making candles just sounds…" He curled his lips in a sour expression.

Blaine chuckled. "I hear you, man. I'm not one to be stuck inside. You can ride out with me—that is, do you know how to ride?"

"I do. My buddy Jonah has horses. Been riding since I was six."

"Good. I can use a strong ranch hand like you. I'll introduce you to my part-timer, Bryce. He just graduated from high school. You'll meet Jim, my full-time cowboy, too. You can help us while your aunt is at the candle shop. I'll pay you, of course."

"Really? You don't have to. It's enough to be here..." Connor's voice faded as he frowned. Then he walked taller as he continued carrying the bin. "Thank you, sir."

"Call me Blaine."

A hint of a smile crossed Connor's face, and Blaine was glad to ease the kid's mind. The two of them continued unloading the back of the vehicle in silence, and when everything was inside, Blaine approached Sienna in the kitchen.

"I'll take you over to the candle shop whenever you're ready. If you'd prefer to unpack and relax, we can go there tomorrow. I have to warn you, though—Mom, Reagan and Holly are practically busting at the seams to see you."

"That's so sweet of them." Her eyes lit up. "Why don't we go over there now?"

Lily bounced over and gave Sienna a side hug. "Can we? I think a candle shop is the coolest thing in the world. I can't wait to see it."

Sienna kissed the side of Lily's head. Blaine wasn't sure what he'd expected from her and the kids, but their obvious closeness wasn't it. They made him want to linger, let some of their bond soak into him, too.

"I'll bring my truck over." Blaine rapped his knuckles on the counter and headed out the door.

The sun warmed his face as he took long strides down the lane. While he wasn't blindsided by the fact that he was still attracted to Sienna, he was surprised to be drawn to her niece and nephew as well. It wasn't as if he lacked family or friends.

Family and friends were fine. They were safe.

He had a brother, two sisters, his mom, dad and four good buddies—plenty of bonding all around. The only person missing was Cody, and Blaine would do about anything to have his little brother back.

Back at his ranch house, Blaine climbed into the driver's seat of the truck and fired up the engine. Sienna's pretty smile plastered itself in his mind as he drove the short distance to the cabin. He was glad she'd be working with his mom and sister. They knew how to support women, unlike him.

Give him a horse, wide-open pastures and the big sky above him. He had cattle to raise, hay to bale, fences to fix and two dogs arriving soon. And that left no time for high school crushes. No time at all.

She'd done the right thing by bringing the kids here for the summer. They needed a break from the chaos at home.

Sienna fought a yawn. After meeting all the Mayer ladies, she and the kids had been given a tour of the candle shop. Blaine's mom, Julie, and his sister, Reagan, made the candles, while his sister-in-law, Holly, managed the business and handled the marketing.

Lily was already enamored with Holly's eighteen-month-old, Clara. Sienna had a feeling her niece would want to babysit the cutie rather than help with candles. Fine by her. After meeting the Mayer clan, she had no doubt they'd welcome Lily's help in watching the child.

Connor, naturally, had hung back with Blaine. Her nephew was on the quiet side, very close to his sister and inclined to outdoor activities. He'd already mentioned he'd talked to Blaine about helping out on the ranch. She wasn't surprised her nephew would prefer ranch work, even mucking stalls, to being around half a dozen women every day.

"You must all be hungry," Julie said. "Kevin's got a big batch of sloppy joes slow-cooking for us. Why don't we head into the house and have some lunch?" She shooed everyone in the direction of the entrance. The group happily chatted all the way to the door.

Sienna fought an overwhelming wave of exhaustion. It had been a long day. A long week. A long year.

This summer getaway was an answer to a prayer. She just hoped God would answer the other prayers heavy on her heart.

The big one concerned her sister, Becca—Connor and Lily's mother. After Aaron, their father, announced he wanted a divorce and proceeded to move out four months ago, Becca had spiraled into a combination of anger, anxiety and bitterness, and it was affecting the kids. No matter how many times Sienna listened to her complain about how unfair the situation was, it wasn't enough. Becca would then unload it all on Connor, too.

Sienna sincerely hoped now that Aaron was ready to reconcile, her sister would stop burdening Connor with her tears and spiteful words about his dad. It wasn't right for her to put that on him.

Julie approached and tilted her head as she asked, "Are you okay?"

Sienna looked around and realized everyone was already outside. She forced her feet forward. "Me? Oh, yes. I'm a bit tired."

"I'm sure. We need to get you off your feet." Julie gave her a warm smile. Blaine's mom was so nice. "We're glad you decided to come spend the summer with us. When Erica mentioned you bringing Connor and Lily, I told her it was exactly what this ranch needs—a couple of teenagers to liven it up. And I don't want you thinking you have to work all the time. We want you to have a nice break before your little one arrives. Do you know what you're having?"

"No, I want it to be a surprise," she replied as they emerged into the sunshine.

"Another thing to look forward to." Julie patted her arm. "How's Erica? I talk to her every day, but it's not the same as seeing her, you know? It's about killing me not being around for her first pregnancy."

"She's good. We had a coffee date last week. Jamie's as busy as ever, and you know your daughter—full of energy." A dart of sadness pierced her heart. She wished she had a mother who wanted to be around for her pregnancy. Her own parents hadn't been in her life for years.

After her brother drowned as a child, their dad left them, and their mom became a shell of her former self. Sienna had been in eighth grade when her mother walked out of her life for good. That's why she'd moved to Sunrise Bend, to live with her grandmother.

Becca, seven years her senior, was living in Germany, where Aaron was stationed. After Grammy died before Sienna's junior year, Becca, Aaron and little Connor returned to Wyoming, and Sienna lived with them until she graduated from high school.

She and Becca were close, and they usually got along great. Her sister had always been prone to anxiety, though, and Sienna was no stranger to helping her through emotional rough patches.

"Erica does have a lot of energy." Julie strolled past potted red petunias and opened the back door of the big house down the lane from the candle shop. "I tell her to rest, but she doesn't listen to me. I'm glad you girls connected. She thinks the world of you."

"I think the world of her, too."

If it wasn't for Erica, Sienna wouldn't have had the chance to get the kids away from their home drama for a few months. She'd shared with her how uncomfortable Becca was making life for Connor. Erica also knew what a drain Sienna's own divorce had been. The offer to stay on the ranch had been a tremendous blessing.

Julie continued through the mudroom to the kitchen, leaving Sienna alone to gather her thoughts, which kept circling back to Blaine.

He was one of a kind. On the quiet side. Easygoing. And kind. So very kind.

She'd been nervous on the way here. What if he'd changed? What if he resented her and the kids staying in his guesthouse? But the instant she'd stepped out of her vehicle, she'd known. Blaine hadn't changed. If anything, he'd gotten better.

And she was a hot mess. Trying to keep everything together while her crumbling life refused to cooperate.

Sienna forced herself to join everyone in the kitchen. Conversation filled the air, along with the tangy aroma of sloppy joes. Connor and Lily both held plates overflowing with food, and her own tummy growled. She fell in line and began filling a plate.

"You and the kids can join us for supper on weeknights." Kevin, a wiry, gray-haired man with twinkling brown eyes, wiped his hands on a kitchen towel. "I cook for a crowd every Monday through Thursday. I'd cook on Friday, too, but Julie here says we have to have date night."

Date night. She loved the thought of them still dating after all these years. "Thank you, Mr. Mayer. We'd love to have supper with you if it's not too much trouble."

"No trouble at all." He beamed. "I'd be offended if you didn't eat with us."

Julie came up next to him. "I'd have asked him to retire years ago if I'd known he was going to whip up feasts all week."

"I didn't know I liked cooking until I retired." He chuckled, then pointed to the counter. "I think we need more napkins, hon."

Turning away, Sienna searched for an empty seat at the long table and set down her plate at the nearest one. After sitting, she took a bite and tried to relax.

She'd always wanted her own big happy family like this one, but it wasn't going to happen. Her ex-husband wouldn't even acknowledge his unborn child. The last time they'd spoken, Troy had informed her he was signing away all parental rights. She didn't even know if he could legally do that. She just hoped he wouldn't do anything drastic, but knowing her ex, she wouldn't be surprised if he did.

She munched on a potato chip. Would she have married him if she'd known him better? Over the past two years, she'd done a lot of research to figure out what was causing his erratic behavior. She was ninety-nine-percent certain he had a personality disorder, not that he'd ever go to a doctor to get diagnosed.

Honestly, at this point, she couldn't even remember why she'd married him. And he must have felt the same, since he'd moved in with his much older girlfriend the day after she told him about the baby. Sienna hadn't realized he'd been cheating on her. But she couldn't say she was surprised.

"Sienna?" Blaine asked.

She blinked. "What? I'm sorry. I didn't hear you."

"Do you want me to drive you guys back after we eat?
I'm sure you want to get settled."

"Yes, I do. Thank you."

She and the kids would unpack, then she was putting
her feet up on the couch and resting for a good hour or
two. Later, she'd take the kids into town for supplies.

One thing she was sure of—Connor and Lily were
going to love Sunrise Bend as much as she did. In fact,
she was going to give them the best summer ever. Becca
and Aaron could work things out back in Casper. Connor and Lily could take their minds off their parents'
problems. And she could rest easy knowing she'd done
all she could to help them. This was the place to do it.

Chapter Two

As Blaine drove Sienna and the kids back to the cabin after lunch, he toyed with the idea of riding out to the re-seeded pasture and checking the new growth. If all went well, he'd be able to cut and bale hay in three weeks. But if the dry conditions continued, he'd have to harvest it sooner.

He wouldn't think about that scenario now. He had enough on his mind.

After he parked the truck, a large SUV kicked up a cloud of dust in the distance. It continued down the long drive before stopping in front of his house.

Tiara and Ollie. Forget checking the pasture. The dogs had arrived.

Laura stepped out. In a faded T-shirt and jeans, she was tall with short gray hair. Blaine loped down the lane to greet her, then gave her his condolences once more.

"Thanks, Blaine. I don't like making Tiara adjust to a new home this late in the pregnancy, but I'm at my wit's end on what else I could do."

"She'll be fine. In fact, she'll feel right at home here in

no time." Blaine glanced over his shoulder. Sienna and the kids had followed him. "Do you guys like dogs?"

"Yeah!" Lily shouted. Connor nodded.

"Well, I'm going to need some help with these two." Blaine hitched his thumb to where Laura was letting the dogs out of the back seat. "Tiara's due to have her puppies this week."

"She's having puppies?" Lily clasped her hands beneath her chin as the beautiful and very pregnant blue-merle Aussie stepped down from the SUV. Laura handed Blaine the leash.

"She sure is." He bent to let Tiara smell the back of his hand, then he stroked the fur on her back and scratched behind her ears. She had a white forehead, chest and front paws. Her back and ears were light gray with black patches, and her blue eyes were surrounded by tan fur. She sure was a beauty.

"Look, Connor, she has blue eyes." Lily pointed to the dog. "How many puppies will she have?"

"The vet thinks at least three." Laura held a leash for Ollie, a gorgeous black tri. The dog was mostly black with white paws, a white chest and tan around his eyes, cheeks and hind legs. Two brown eyes looked up at Blaine as if to say "pet me, too."

"He's a looker, isn't he?" Blaine took his leash.

"Yes, their previous litter was colorful." Laura gave the dogs a bittersweet smile. "It will be interesting to see the variety of pups in this one."

Anticipation rushed through him as it all came back—gathering supplies, checking her temperature and, when she was ready to deliver, the wonder of watching each tiny pup come into the world.

"Is there any way you can keep Ollie away from her

for a few weeks after she gives birth? I don't want him bothering her. They get along great, but she'll have enough on her mind without his energetic self. I can take him back with me if need be."

"We can keep Ollie with us." Lily, all bright-eyed and hopeful, was petting him, and the dog lapped up the attention. "If it's alright with you, Aunt Sienna."

Blaine straightened. She seemed fine with the idea. "We'd love to have him."

"Ollie should stay with Tiara until she's ready to deliver," Laura said. "Dad trained both to herd, so don't be afraid to use him around the ranch."

Blaine gestured to the kids. "After Tiara has the puppies, Ollie can sleep in the cabin with you guys. In the meantime, he'll stay with me."

"That would be great." Connor crouched down and ruffled the fur on Ollie's head.

"Won't she miss him after she has the puppies?" Lily chewed her lower lip.

"She'll have too much on her mind to worry about Ollie during the first week or two after having her puppies." Laura gestured for Lily to come around the rear of the vehicle, where she lifted the back hatch. "We're going to set up a whelping box for her in one of Blaine's rooms. I brought everything Tiara will need. Why don't you help me get this stuff inside?"

"Do you mind holding them for a minute?" Blaine handed the leashes to Sienna. Their hands touched, and the feel of her soft skin whispered sensations up his arm. How could a simple touch be so disorienting?

"I don't mind at all." She met his gaze, and he was transported back to being sixteen, hanging on her every word but too shy to do anything about it.

"That's a lot of stuff." Lily poked around the boxes.

"Tell me about it." Laura grabbed a stack of folders and waved them to Blaine. "Here are their papers, vet records and the breeding book Dad used."

Blaine sprang into action, stacking the folders onto one of the bins and hauling it out of her vehicle. It didn't take long to move everything into his house. Once the back was unloaded, he told Laura he'd see her at the funeral. She gave Tiara and Ollie a final goodbye, swallowed hard and drove away.

"Well, guys," Sienna said, handing the leashes back to Blaine. "I'm getting pretty tired. Why don't we unpack and then go into town for supplies?"

Connor and Lily exchanged a glance.

"Go ahead and take a nap, Aunt Sienna," Connor said. "We're going to help get the dogs settled."

"You can see them later." She arched her eyebrows. "You need to unpack."

"Okay. We'll unpack." Lily sighed grudgingly before turning to Blaine. "Mr. Mayer, do you want us to help get Tiara's things organized once we're done?"

"You can call me Blaine, Lily." He was enjoying the teens. "And, yes, I could use some help."

He didn't really need help. He remembered exactly how Ralph's room had been set up for deliveries. But Lily seemed so eager and happy, it made him want to keep her eager and happy.

"Yay! We'll unpack our stuff and come over, right, Connor?"

"Can Ollie come to the cabin with us?" Connor's eyes met Blaine's.

"Why don't you let me give him a tour of my house with Tiara first? This is going to be a new experience for both of them, and it will be easier for them to be together right now." Then he turned to Tiara. "Are you ready, girl? Let's get you inside. You can check out your new home."

"Okay." Connor gave Ollie one more longing look. "We'll be over as soon as we unpack."

Blaine glanced at Sienna. "If you need anything, call or text me." He'd given her his number at lunch.

"I will." The three of them turned and headed back to the cabin, leaving him, Ollie and Tiara standing in his driveway.

"Come on, you two. We'd better get the whelping box set up. We don't want those pups of yours arriving without everything prepared." Blaine led the dogs up the walkway to his house. Both were alert, sniffing the grass as they went along. Inside, he unhooked their leashes and let them roam around. He watched Tiara carefully. She was heavy with puppies, but she didn't seem uncomfortable or out of sorts. In fact, her curiosity kept her moving at a rapid pace.

He followed them from room to room, mentally deciding where he would set up the dog nursery. The spare bedroom next to his was the best option. It had a comfortable bed where he could sleep those first nights after she had the pups, and it had plenty of space for him to set up her supplies.

Blaine put together the whelping box and lined it with some of the soft blankets Laura had provided. He was glad to see Ralph had upgraded to a box with a pig rail— a protector rail—to keep the newborns from accidentally being smothered by their mom. To his surprise, Tiara walked right into it, circled twice, lied down and fell asleep. It wasn't easy being a pregnant dog, evidently.

Ollie stayed close to Blaine as he hauled the rest of

the bins into the room, stacked towels next to the dresser, put piles of soft blankets in one of the drawers and arranged all the necessary supplies on top of the dresser. He flipped through the breeding journal, noting the details of her pregnancy.

A knock at the front door had him clamoring to his feet and hurrying down the hall. On his doorstep, Connor and Lily were grinning.

"Where is she?" Lily asked. "Did she have the puppies yet?"

Connor rolled his eyes but didn't say anything.

"Not yet. According to Ralph's breeding journal, it should be toward the end of the week."

Ollie zoomed straight to Connor, then sat at his feet and looked up at him. The shimmer in Connor's eyes as he petted the dog told Blaine everything he needed to know. The kid already loved Ollie.

Blaine didn't blame him. He loved dogs, too. The ranch always had an array of working canines on it, and Jim's border collie, Ringo, rode out with them every day. It would be good to have another dog helping herd the cattle.

"Come on, I'll take you to Tiara's room." Blaine gestured for them to follow him. "Is your aunt doing alright?"

"Yeah, she fell asleep on the couch." Lily skipped over. Ollie ran ahead and Connor joined them.

Blaine took them past the living room and kitchen, then down the hall to the spare room where Tiara was now sitting up, tail wagging, as Ollie sniffed her ear.

"Aww, look, they love each other," Lily said.

"Do you think he'll be okay with us in the cabin?" Connor asked Blaine. "I mean, after she has the puppies?

He's always lived with her, and he'll have to get used to sleeping in a strange place by himself."

Connor would have to get used to sleeping in a strange place, too, and Blaine wondered if the kid missed home, if he was nervous about staying at the ranch for weeks on end.

"I think he'll be okay. But maybe he could sleep in your room if you're worried."

Lily's face fell, and Blaine realized his mistake. "Or you two could take turns."

He didn't see how that would work, but he didn't know what else to say. This was why he tried not to get involved in other people's business.

"It's okay." She lifted her chin. "Once the puppies are born, I'm going to have to spend a lot of time with them, so Ollie can stay in your room, Connor."

Blaine hadn't expected that. "Do you want to be here when she gives birth?"

"I'm not sure." Lily's nose scrunched. "I mean, yeah, it would be cool to be there, but I don't know. Will it be bloody?"

"There are a few drops here and there. Mostly, Tiara will be shaking and panting between puppies."

"What's all this stuff for?" Lily drifted over to the dresser, noting the thermometer and all the other supplies.

Blaine explained what everything was used for, and she nodded eagerly throughout, asking lots of questions.

"Here's the breeding book I mentioned." Blaine pointed to the folders. "You might want to check it out."

"Yoo-hoo, I'm coming in." Sienna's voice carried from the front hall.

Lily raced out of the room and yelled, "Aunt Sienna, you have to see this!"

Blaine hitched his chin at Connor. "It might be weird staying here for the first couple of nights. I'm sure you miss your house and parents and friends."

He swallowed nervously. "Yeah, but it's fine. Like Aunt Sienna said, it's an adventure."

"You've got a good attitude." Blaine clapped his hand on Connor's shoulder. "If you want to loaf around for a few days—enjoy some summer vacation—I don't mind."

"No." He shook his head rapidly. "I want to help."

"Okay. Ollie will come with us. A good herding dog is worth his weight in gold on a ranch."

"How do you train a dog to herd?" Connor seemed to have a whole new appreciation for Ollie, who was snooping around the box in the corner.

Before he could answer, Lily dragged Sienna by the hand into the room. "See? It's Tiara's own pregnancy ward. Doesn't she look happy?"

"She does. What a great place for her to have her babies." Sienna's skin was flushed and her hair less tidy than before. She glanced at Blaine. "I hate to break up the party, but we really need to get some groceries."

"No problem." His voice was as gravelly as the driveway.

"I don't want to leave Ollie." Connor looked concerned. "It's his first day here."

"And Blaine's going to let me look at the breeding book." Lily's eyes pleaded with her aunt.

"They can stay here while you shop," Blaine said. "I don't mind."

"If that's what you guys want…" She gave them all a smile that didn't quite reach her eyes. "I'll just run into town and grab a few things. I'll be back before you know it."

"Okay," Connor said. "Hey, would you mind getting some beef jerky?"

"And gummy bears," Lily added.

"Got it." She took out her phone and made a note to herself before looking up. "Anything else?"

Connor and Lily walked her to the front door, telling her their requests, and then she opened it and waved to them both. Blaine stood behind the kids and watched her as she climbed into her vehicle. He continued staring as the kids turned their attention back to the dogs.

All that familiar red hair and those flashing dimples brought up questions. Like why was she divorced? And how could a man let a woman like her walk away?

Blaine had purposely *not* asked his mother or Erica any questions about Sienna. Figured it would be better that way. The less he probed, the easier it would be to remain detached. But now he wondered...

He closed the door and turned to Lily. "Let me get you that breeding book."

Ditched by her own kin. Sienna drove down Main Street and, on a whim, went right on by Big Buck Supermarket to see if downtown Sunrise Bend had changed much in the years she'd been gone. How many times had she longed to drive back? To see her old friends? To soak in the town where she'd felt so at home during a terrible time in her life?

But she'd never gotten the nerve to come back. She'd lost contact with her high school friends years ago, and part of her had always worried that her memories were sugarcoated, better than the real thing. The reality of

Sunrise Bend in the present might spoil her sweet view of the past.

She slowed her vehicle as she reached downtown. The candy shop was still there. A few new stores had opened, and one of them caught her attention. Brewed Awakening?

Coffee? *Yes, please!*

Sienna eased the compact SUV into one of the angled parking spots in front of the coffee shop. If this place made decaf blended iced coffees, she'd be the happiest woman alive.

The baby kicked as Sienna stepped onto the pavement. Probably could sense the coffee coming soon. Smart child. She rubbed her belly affectionately.

Her life was messy at the moment, but this baby was the best thing she could ever imagine. She just wished it would have a father in its life. There was still a chance Troy wouldn't be rash and give up his parental rights. But even if he didn't, she had no illusions about him being a steady presence in their child's life. He was too erratic. She didn't see that changing.

She went inside and waited in line behind two older women. The interior was not the rustic affair she'd expected in a town like this. It was bright, modern and comfortable. She could see herself coming here often. In fact, a slideshow of future snapshots that were never going to happen rolled through her brain. Her carrying her baby inside at Christmastime for a coffee break. Sipping an iced brew while holding the toddler's hand in the summer. Getting a hot chocolate together after school in the fall.

"May I help you?" A striking brunette wiped her hands

down her denim apron. She was wearing a form-fitting black T-shirt and a necklace with a bird charm.

"Do you sell decaf blended iced coffee?"

"Yes, we do. What flavor can I get you?"

"Salted caramel, please."

"Coming right up." The woman turned away to make the drink, and Sienna scolded herself. Maybe her penchant for living in fantasyland was why she hadn't ever made the trip back to Sunrise Bend. One second in this coffee shop had been all it took to picture a rosy future for her and her baby here.

But she didn't have a future here. And she couldn't let herself forget it.

Two months. Then she'd be driving back to Casper, praying Becca and Aaron had worked things out, and resuming her normal life, albeit alone.

A bell above the door chimed. "Hey, Bridget."

Sienna turned to see who was speaking. A woman holding a small boy's hand came up to the register. Sienna scooted down to the end of the counter to give them space. She couldn't help peeking at the boy, likely three or four, with dark hair, brown eyes and a big toothy grin. He was adorable.

"Oh, hey, guys." The woman behind the counter— Bridget, obviously—looked over her shoulder from where she was making the drink. "And how is Tucker today?"

"Mama's taking me to the candle store. I have to be gentle with Cwara." His lisp was the cutest thing ever.

The candle store. They must be headed to Mayer Canyon Candles. The thought of working there, even part-time, filled her with cheer. The ladies all seemed fun and professional. She was really looking forward to spending time with them and doing something creative for a change.

"That sounds fun." Bridget injected excitement in her voice. "I know you'll be very gentle with Clara." He nodded solemnly. She turned her attention to his mother. "How's your dad doing, Tess?"

"Not good…"

Tess… Sienna drew her eyebrows together. She vaguely remembered a girl named Tess a few years younger than her. The two women finished their conversation, and Bridget handed Sienna her drink.

"Wait, are you Sienna?" Tess's jaw dropped and her brown eyes began to sparkle. "I'd recognize that gorgeous red hair anywhere. You probably don't remember me. I moved here not long before you moved away, and I was a few grades behind you."

"I do remember you." Sienna tucked away the compliment and pushed a straw into the lid. She didn't always love her red hair, and to hear it described as gorgeous was nice indeed. "It looks like you've been busy. Is this your little boy?"

"This is Tucker. He's three." Tess lovingly smoothed his hair. "And I have another one on the way. I see you've been busy, too." She grinned, pointing to Sienna's baby bump.

"How wonderful. Yes, I'm due at the end of August."

"It's baby season." Bridget, busy with Tess's order, gave them a backward glance. "I guarantee Holly gets pregnant soon."

"They've only been married for two months." Tess shook her head.

"So? There are babies in the air around here lately."

"I can't argue with you about that," Tess said. Then

she turned to Sienna. "By the way, this is Bridget Renna, soon to be Bridget Tolbert. Do you remember Mac? They're engaged." Tess's eyebrows soared as if it was the best news ever.

"How exciting!" Sienna added just enough enthusiasm into her tone. She did remember Mac. Cute, rich, nice. He'd never been her type, though, and she was absolutely sure she'd never been his, either. Looking at Tess and Bridget, she couldn't help feeling they had their lives together, while hers had fallen apart. "Congratulations."

"Thank you." A smile brightened Bridget's face. "It's hard to believe how much my life has changed in the past six months."

"I hear you," Sienna said almost under her breath.

"So what brings you back?" Tess asked Sienna.

"I'm working part-time at Mayer Canyon Candles until the end of July. My nephew, Connor—he's sixteen—and my niece, Lily, who is thirteen, are with me. Erica offered to let us spend the next two months in one of the empty cabins."

"And your husband's okay with that?" Tess teased.

"We're no longer together." Sienna pushed away the bitterness those words brought up. "We got divorced."

Tess's face fell as she exchanged a glance with Bridget. "I'm so sorry—I had no idea. What a dumb thing to say."

"It's okay."

Bridget faced Sienna then. "Are you staying on Jet's property or Blaine's?"

"Blaine's." Sienna could have hugged her for changing the subject.

"Oh, good," Tess said with enthusiasm.

Why was that good?

"You'll have to join us the next time we have a Friday night get-together." Bridget handed Tess the two to-go cups. "You can bring your niece and nephew. I'm sure Kaylee would love to meet them."

"Kaylee?" Sienna asked.

"Sorry, I've gotten so used to everyone knowing everyone around here—Kaylee is Mac's sister. She's sixteen."

"Oh, yeah, that would be great." She'd worried about Connor and Lily being isolated at the ranch. "I'm sure they would love to meet her. Although, they're both currently obsessed with Blaine's new dogs."

"New dogs?" Tess took a sip.

"Yeah, they arrived a couple hours ago. Both Australian shepherds. The female is pregnant. I think he took them in as a favor. A woman dropped them off while we were there."

"I'm heading to the candle shop now to discuss their invoicing system," Tess said. "I'll find out the scoop on the dogs."

"Oh, do you work there, too?" Sienna asked.

"I own a bookkeeping service. They're one of my clients. I love it because it gives me an excuse to hang out with them whenever I need a break from everything."

"The candle shop is amazing."

"That it is."

"Well, I'd better get going. I'm sure I'll be seeing you around." Sienna gave them both a smile, waved to Tucker and headed to the door. She hadn't expected everyone to be so friendly. And in the years that she'd been away, she'd forgotten how towns this small worked. Everyone seemed to know everyone else. Along with everything about them.

Which meant it was only a matter of time before the entire town knew she was divorced and about to be a single mom.

Sighing, she got back into her car and set the iced coffee, which was delicious, into the cup holder. People knowing her business didn't bother her. It wasn't as if she could change anything. But Connor and Lily... She didn't want anyone gossiping about them. Especially not about Connor. Her nephew often grew quiet and withdrawn after talking to his mom. If Becca would just stop dumping her problems on him...

Being away would help. Sienna wanted him to have a carefree summer.

After starting the vehicle, she let it idle and sipped her drink. She'd be there for Lily and Connor, the way she always had. She'd promised herself long ago that she'd be their rock. And nothing would change that.

He hadn't thought this through. He needed to get a plan in place for the Tiara situation.

The following morning, Blaine helped Tiara and Ollie into the back seat of his truck. The day was warm, without a lick of moisture in the air. He kept praying for rain, but it never showed up.

He drove the truck down the long driveway leading out to the main road. Earlier he'd taken Tiara's temperature—100.4 degrees, which was good since it meant she wasn't approaching labor. But when she did go into labor, he was going to have to drop everything to help her deliver the puppies. He would also need to watch her and the newborns closely the first week, which meant someone else would need to take care of the cattle.

His full-timer, Jim, was capable of handling the ranch

duties during the day, and his part-timer, Bryce, worked every morning. Blaine planned on speaking to them both later about taking on extra duties once the puppies arrived. In the meantime, he couldn't leave Tiara alone when she was this close to giving birth.

His mom would know what to do.

Blaine turned onto the road leading to the other side of the ranch. The pastures spread out for miles. He passed Jet and Holly's new house, then his parents' house, and parked in front of the pole barn, where the candle business was housed.

He held open the door for the dogs to exit out of the back seat, then led them both into the showroom, where Holly and Reagan were standing in the kitchen area, laughing and sipping from mugs. Little Clara was pulling on Holly's pant leg. Mom was nowhere to be seen.

Although this was his family, he avoided coming into the candle shop as much as possible. The gang of Mayer women always asked him questions he didn't know how to answer. None of the questions were about things he actually wanted to discuss, like the new calves or how the reseeded pasture was growing. No, they asked things like had he noticed Janelle wasn't sitting next to Richie in church? And then they'd suggest Blaine should call her. Blech.

Janelle was not his type.

Red hair and dimples were.

Stop thinking about Sienna. It's a dead end.

"Blaine!" Reagan face lit up. His sister was five years younger than him. A dreamer and very creative, she had a big heart. "I heard you're having puppies."

"Well, not me personally." He grinned as she crouched to pet Tiara, then Ollie. "This one here is, though."

"Can I get a ride with you to the funeral tomorrow?" Reagan asked, straightening.

"Yeah. Are Mom and Dad coming, too?"

She nodded. "But they want to go to the outfitter shop after, and I cannot stand around for an hour while Dad touches every saddle. I have my limits."

He chuckled. "Point taken."

Holly, carrying Clara, approached and pointed to the dogs. "See the doggies?"

"Woof, woof," Clara said, twisting in her arms and clapping.

"You know she's going to adore them." Holly lowered her to the floor, keeping her arms circled around the child. The dogs sniffed Clara, causing her to giggle. Holly sighed. "I am *not* ready for a puppy yet."

"Don't worry. You have plenty of time for a dog or two when she's older." Blaine doted on his niece. After handing the leashes to Reagan, he scooped up Clara into his arms and tweaked her nose. "You like the dogs?"

"Woof, woof." She beamed at him, placing her chubby palms on both his cheeks.

"You're getting pretty smart, little lady."

She smooshed his cheeks together. He couldn't help but laugh.

His mom came through the workshop door and made a beeline to him. "My, my, Tiara looks ready to pop, doesn't she?" She gently stroked the dog's fur, and Tiara's tail wagged.

"Yeah, about that. I'm in a bit of a bind." He handed Clara back to Holly. "I can't keep an eye on Tiara while I'm checking cattle."

"Oh, don't worry." Mom waved off his concerns. "Your dad will pick her up first thing in the morning and bring her to our house. He'll be glad to watch her for you. If he thinks she's close to going into labor, he'll give you a call."

Blaine was taken aback. Of course. Problem solved.

Why hadn't he thought of asking his dad? The man was retired and had time on his hands. Probably because after Cody died, Dad had withdrawn in his grief, and Blaine had been uncomfortable around him. He'd gotten in the habit of not asking for his father's help, but it was time to change that.

"Should I go over there now and ask him?" Blaine jerked his thumb to the door.

"It wouldn't hurt. Take the dogs, too. Then Tiara will be able to nose around the house and get used to being there." Mom pivoted toward the kitchen area. "Have time for a cup of coffee first?"

He debated escaping. He'd made it this long without any hints about getting a girlfriend. Why push it?

Mom's eager eyes did him in, though. She loved it when he stopped over, and he hated letting her down.

"Sure." He followed her and dragged out a stool from under the counter to sit on. The dogs had their noses down and were smelling around the space with Reagan patiently holding their leashes. Holly took Clara over to her desk, where there was an adjacent play area.

"How is Sienna settling in, poor thing?" Behind the counter, Mom poured him a cup and slid the mug his way.

"Why do you say 'poor thing'?"

"Well, it can't be easy on her." She eyed him over the rim of her mug.

"Coming here for the summer with her niece and nephew?" He wasn't sure what Mom was getting at.

"No, Blaine, I'm talking about being pregnant and divorced. It's scary. But, yes, I give her a lot of credit for taking her niece and nephew for the summer. That isn't easy, either."

Sienna made it look easy. She made it look like she'd been a mother figure to both kids all their lives. They loved her, and she loved them. It was obvious.

"Just be extra gentle with her." Mom gave him *the look*. He wanted to roll his eyes like a sixth grader and give her a snotty *okay*.

"I will." To be honest, he didn't plan on spending much time with Sienna. He was busy with the ranch. She'd be working here, and when she wasn't, she'd be with Connor and Lily. There really wasn't much reason for them to interact.

"I mean it. Look out for her. She's got too much on her plate right now. We need to support her."

"Got it." But did he? How much support was he supposed to give? He wasn't even sure what his mother meant. He didn't want to know, either.

At least they were in agreement about Sienna deserving to be treated gently. He had no problem with that. But he still didn't plan on spending any more time with her than was necessary. His attraction to her hadn't faded, and she wasn't in any condition for a relationship. Why put himself through the pain of wanting something he couldn't have? He knew better than to get too close to a fire.

Chapter Three

It was time to give up on her hopes that her sister would stop calling Connor to cry and complain about Aaron. Didn't Becca understand Connor was her son and not her therapist? He shouldn't have to hear bad things about his dad. It wasn't right.

No matter how many times Sienna had gently asked Becca to stop dumping her problems on Connor, her sister wouldn't listen.

So much for her great plan of out of sight, out of mind.

Sienna slipped out of the cabin and quietly shut the front door behind her Thursday morning. So far, staying at the ranch had been great. In the three days they'd been here, Connor was smiling more often and playing with Ollie. He acted like any other sixteen-year-old boy would. But last night Sienna had overheard him talking to his mom, and he'd returned to serious mode again.

It infuriated her when Becca did this.

Maybe she should talk to her sister again about boundaries. Sienna was the one Becca usually turned to for emotional support. She no longer allowed her to cry or repeat the same complaints for hours anymore. It was too draining. And she didn't want Connor dealing with it, either.

Trying to shake off her nerves, she headed to the lane leading to the stables. The kids were sleeping in, and she'd been watching the comings and goings of the ranch enough since arriving to know Blaine would be riding back to the stables soon. She didn't have a clue as to what he did all day, but she did know the first hours of his mornings were spent on horseback.

The sun cast a glow on the sparse grass, flaxen in color due to the lack of rain. Normally, she'd soak in the view of the prairie and cattle grazing, but she had a lot on her mind.

Was it wise to tell Blaine what was going on with Connor? She kept her private life…private. And this was Connor's life, not hers. At this point, though, she felt it was necessary. Blaine spent hours with her nephew every afternoon, and he needed to know what Connor was going through, the pressure he was under. That way he wouldn't inadvertently make her nephew's problems worse.

Plus, she didn't want him misconstruing Connor's silence as defiance or rudeness.

The pounding of hooves made her pause. Right on time. Her breath caught at seeing Blaine on the large quarter horse with white forelegs. Ollie trotted alongside him.

What a cowboy.

He was handsome and rugged and everything she found attractive in a man, especially wearing that cowboy hat, a short-sleeved shirt, jeans, chaps and cowboy boots. Those blue eyes and dark blond hair were heart-stopping enough. His tanned arms were corded with muscles he'd earned working on the ranch. He was a sight that would brighten any woman's day.

Too bad she had no business looking. Had it slipped her mind that she was fresh off a divorce and pregnant? Maybe he had a pair of blinders in the stables she could borrow. The last thing she should be doing was checking out Blaine Mayer.

Her attraction was a dead end. She belonged in Casper, near Connor and Lily and Becca.

Blaine slowed the horse, dismounted and, with the reins in his hand, strode over to her. Ollie joined them, and she petted the dog.

"Is something wrong?" He frowned, wiping his forehead right below his hat. "Are you feeling okay?"

"Nothing's wrong." It was so kind of him to ask how she was feeling. His mom, Holly and Reagan asked her often, too. She appreciated their concern. "I was hoping you'd have a minute. I wanted to discuss something with you."

His frown deepened. "Of course. Let me deal with Boots and I'll be right back."

She waited while he led the horse through the stables. He called out, "Bryce, would you come here a minute?"

The baby chose that moment to kick, and a shot of joy eased her worries. The rest of her life might be complicated, but having this child wasn't.

"Okay, I'm all yours." His face grew red. "I mean, I'm ready to talk. Or listen." His jaw shifted. "Let's go to the backyard. There's a bench swing. It'll be more comfortable than standing."

"Sure." The simple act of strolling next to him brought back a batch of memories and impressions. "Do you remember when we all went to the rodeo? Allie, Luke and

Morgan ditched us, and you and I spent an hour combing the place for them."

He glanced at her, grinning. "Yeah, and we finally gave up and bought French fries and iced lemonades."

"They were delicious. And we actually watched the rodeo."

"They acted surprised when they caught up with us later."

"Did they really think we hadn't noticed they'd been gone half the day?" She laughed. "It was a good thing they took their time. I was so mad when we were trying to find them. I probably would have given them a piece of my mind and regretted it later. You were the one who said we should grab something to eat and not let them ruin our day."

"I did?"

"Yes, and I've never forgotten it."

His steps faltered. Sienna glanced his way, then mentally shrugged as he fell back into his easy stride. His backyard came into view, and he gestured to the wooden bench swing. The frame had been mounted on a concrete slab almost flush with the lawn.

"Have a seat," he said.

She did, although none too gracefully. Ollie sprawled out on the lawn, and Blaine leaned his forearm on the frame, watching her. It made her cheeks feel warm, so she patted the seat. "Why don't you sit down, too?" And not stare at her. She couldn't take the scrutiny.

"Nah, I'm good." Was that fear in his eyes? Couldn't be. Not this big, strong cowboy.

"I wanted to talk to you about Connor." She wrapped her arms under her stomach, clasping her hands lightly.

A breeze tickled the hair around her face. She loved the warmth of summer after long, harsh Wyoming winters.

"Something wrong?"

"No." She shook her head. "He's, well… He can be…" Why did confiding in Blaine feel like she was inviting him to either criticize her or get close to her? She wanted to have an easy friendship with him—like when they were younger—but letting him in on the realities of her life and Connor's felt intimate. Too intimate.

A deep wrinkle formed in his forehead. "Is there something I should be worried about?"

"Yes. Well, not worried, exactly." She blew out a breath. "He's on the quiet side, and I don't want you to get the wrong impression."

"So he doesn't talk much." Blaine shrugged. "No big deal. I'm older, technically his boss and he doesn't really know me."

"I have a feeling he'll be quiet today, and he can come across as sullen, but he isn't. He just has a lot to deal with."

"Like what?"

She hesitated a moment. "One of the reasons I brought him and Lily here was so he could have some separation from what's going on at home. Their mom—Becca—is my sister. I love her dearly, and I don't want you to think I'm bad-mouthing her, but Aaron, their father, left about four months ago, saying he wanted a divorce."

"I'm sorry to hear that." His blue eyes shimmered with sympathy.

"It shocked her. He wasn't having an affair or anything. I don't know exactly what happened. All I know is my sister didn't handle it well and started confiding in Connor, often crying or complaining about Aaron."

He winced.

"No matter how many times I tell her—as gently as possible, of course—that she's putting her son in a difficult position and it's not fair for him to be in the middle, she doesn't stop."

"Does he ever see his dad?"

"They always had a decent relationship before Aaron left, but they haven't spent any time together since the breakup. And I'm hoping… Well, Aaron is in Casper now with my sister. They're trying to work things out."

"Ahh." A look of understanding crossed his face. "You're giving them space. That's why you're here."

His response was why it was dangerous to get close to him. He was perceptive and understanding, which tempted her to lean on him. But every man she'd ever leaned on had let her down. Walked away. As if she'd meant nothing to them.

She couldn't face that kind of rejection again.

"Yes, but it's more." She forced herself back to the issue at hand. "I brought Lily and Connor here so they could be normal teens for a few months, away from the drama of their home life. The thing about my sister, though, is she's either hot or cold. When she's happy, everyone's happy. When she's miserable, she repeats her troubles to anyone who will listen, including her son. And she can't always see clearly."

"That must be frustrating."

It was. In fact, it upset her and made her sad. She'd spent hour after hour listening to her sister spewing about what a jerk Aaron was and crying about being left to fend for herself. Sienna had held Becca's hand, hugged her and brought takeout to eat with her night after night. For months she'd been wound tight with worry thinking about Lily and Connor dealing with the divorce. And this had been when she'd been dealing with her own divorce. It had been a rough year.

No matter how much emotional support Sienna gave, Becca needed more. From everyone. And she was so self-involved when things were bad, she couldn't see how it affected the loved ones around her.

"Yeah, well, it's hard to keep up with her," Sienna said. "One day Aaron is the biggest jerk who ever lived, and the next day she's ecstatic because he reached out and held her hand on their way to couples' therapy. It's like being the passenger on an emotional roller coaster. But you can never get off. I don't want Connor dealing with it."

Blaine rubbed his chin, his gaze off in the distance.

She'd said way more than she should have. Way more than she'd intended.

"You don't want me to talk to him about it." The way he said it was a declaration, not a question, and it was a relief that he understood without her having to spell it out.

"No, I don't," she said. "I just don't want you to be surprised if Connor seems down. He's not being surly or disrespectful, I can promise you that. These conversations with his mom tend to throw him in a funk."

A breeze waved between them. The scents of earth and fresh air tickled her nose. Blaine appeared to be lost in thought.

"I guess we'll have to help him." He faced her, adjusting the rim of his cowboy hat.

"Oh, no." She shook her head. "This isn't your problem."

"What were we doing in the summer when we were sixteen?" His eyes seemed to drink her in, and she blushed, uncertain where the conversation was headed.

"Getting pizza, riding horses, hopping on four-wheelers, going to the rodeo and any other local attraction that pulled into town." She had fond memories of those days. They'd been the most carefree ones she'd ever experienced.

"Then let's make sure Connor and Lily have the same thing."

There he went again, using the word *we*.

"I appreciate what you're saying, Blaine, but I've imposed too much already." She didn't want him to think she was ungrateful, but Connor and Lily were her responsibility, not his. "You don't have to do anything. I just thought it was important for you to know what's going on. That's it."

She couldn't have asked for a better response from Blaine, but it was dangerous accepting his help. Sixteen was a lifetime ago, and reliving it with Blaine, Lily and Connor might make her want more.

She'd been blessed to enjoy it once. Happiness like that didn't come around twice.

Blaine ground the heel of his boot into the dirt. He'd read that situation wrong. As usual.

He shouldn't have suggested getting involved.

Staring at Sienna's profile as she gently moved the swing back and forth with one sandal-clad foot, he had the odd sensation of having done this before. Not watching Sienna swing—no, having someone he cared about confide in him, then refuse to let him get involved.

Cody.

A flare of unexpected sadness hit him hard.

Blaine had tucked this particular memory deep down, tried to smother it until it disappeared, but it was still there, oozing guilt out of the seams of a patchwork pocket where he'd buried it.

His brother had been about Connor's age when he'd bragged to Blaine about drinking with older kids out at the flats. Blaine could still see the excitement in Cody's eyes. He'd told him not to hang out with those guys, that they were bad news. Cody had laughed it off, told him to lighten up, that if he wanted a lecture he'd have told Dad or Jet.

Those were the words that had stopped Blaine from doing the right thing. He'd liked the fact Cody had confided in him and not Jet. Everyone always went to Jet first.

But not that time.

And because of it, he'd kept Cody's secret.

If Blaine had done the right thing and told his parents, they would have kept Cody from hanging out with those guys. Then his brother wouldn't have wasted the next years of his life high and drunk, ultimately leaving the ranch in a whirlwind of anger.

And Blaine would have been able to tell him how much he meant to him before the car accident that took his life.

Sienna stopped swinging, gripped the armrest and heaved herself to a standing position.

"Thanks for listening." She smiled. "I'd better get back."

"Wait." He wished he had time to think this through, to talk himself out of what he was about to suggest, but if he waited, he'd make the wrong choice. Just like he had with Cody all those years ago. "I know we can't change what's going on in Connor's life. His mom's going to call him, and he's going to talk to her. It's what parents and kids do. But maybe if he had things to look forward to all summer, it would help take his mind off the problems back home."

Her pretty green eyes gleamed as she digested what he was saying.

He said a silent prayer. *God, I know it's dicey getting involved with Sienna, considering we're not in a position to have a relationship, but my gut is telling me not to slink into the shadows on this one.*

"What kinds of things?"

She was actually open to his suggestion? He was surprised.

"The same things you mentioned." He rubbed the back of his neck. "Riding horses and four-wheelers, getting pizza, going to the rodeo. There's a big Fourth of July festival every year."

"Hmm...but we were hanging out with our friends. He only has Lily."

"He has you, too." Blaine tilted his head. He belatedly remembered how packed the next eight weeks would be. He'd be cutting and baling hay sometime in June, putting the bulls out to pasture with the cows soon after... and then there were the puppies.

Promising to give Connor and Lily a fun summer with Sienna might be tougher than he thought.

"Mac's sister, Kaylee, would probably introduce him to some of the teens." He shifted his weight from one foot to the other.

"Even if she does, I don't know if he'd feel comfortable with new people so quickly." She tapped her chin. "I think you're right, though. I've been trying to get Becca to stop calling him with her problems, and she's clearly not going to. Maybe having some distractions would help. When's the next rodeo?"

"There's one every Friday if you don't mind driving half an hour to it." Excitement sprouted as he thought about spending more time with Sienna and the kids.

He should *not* be getting excited. Couldn't be, really.

She was only here for the summer.

She was having a baby.

Moving back to Casper.

And he'd still be here, trying to bring new life to a dead pasture and growing his herd. But he couldn't turn his back on Connor. He had to follow his instincts. He'd ignored them all those years ago out of pride. He wasn't ignoring them now.

His phone buzzed. He took it out of his pocket—Dad was calling.

"What's up?" he asked.

"Tiara's temperature dropped."

"I'll be right there." He ended the call and turned to Sienna. "I've got to pick up Tiara."

Her grin spread, looking as radiant as the sunrise. "Does this mean...?"

"Yep. It looks like we're having puppies tonight." Whether he was ready for them or not.

It was her phone's turn to buzz. She checked it and grimaced.

"What's wrong?"

"Nothing." The way her lips puckered told him it wasn't nothing. She rubbed her forearms as they made their way to the front yard. Then she hitched her chin in the direction of the cabin. "I'll let the kids know today's the day."

"Are you sure everything's alright?"

"It's fine," she said curtly. "It's nothing. My ex. That's all."

Her ex.

He watched her walk to the cabin until she was half-way there.

She hadn't been divorced for long. And she was carrying the guy's child.

Did her ex want to get back together? Did she?

All the more reason for him to guard his heart. Getting close to her wouldn't be fair to either of them. He'd keep his focus where it belonged—on the ranch, the puppies and giving the teens a summer to remember. Good or bad, he had a feeling he'd be remembering it for years to come.

Chapter Four

"Why hasn't she had them yet?" Lily asked Blaine later that afternoon. He'd been in the spare room with her and Tiara for hours. Sienna and Connor had grown tired of waiting and had taken Ollie outside to play. Every so often they'd pop in to ask how it was going, and his answer was always the same. *Nothing yet.*

"Just be patient." If he had a dollar for every time he'd said those words today...

"Do you think something's wrong?" She was kneeling on the floor next to the whelping box, where Tiara was panting heavily.

"No. This is just how nature works. When the first pup is ready, it will come out. And then she'll have the remaining puppies every fifteen to thirty minutes until they're all born."

Blaine had to hand it to Lily; she was adamant about being here no matter what. Whenever Sienna checked on them, she asked Lily if she wanted to take a break, and the girl always shook her head. It reminded Blaine of his first go-round helping Ralph deliver puppies. Nothing could have dragged him away.

He checked his phone again. Jim had called earlier to let him know the herd was fine, but a section of fence needed to be repaired in one of the far pastures. The wheatgrass wasn't ready to be cut yet, so Tiara giving birth today was the best timing he could have asked for.

"Are you sure nothing's wrong?" Lily sat back and hugged her knees to her chest. "Why is she doing that?"

He studied the dog more carefully. Tiara was licking herself, and he could see her belly contracting.

"You know what? I think she's about ready." He pointed to the dog's stomach. "See how it's moving?"

Lily scrambled to her knees. "Oh, yes, I see it." Her voice trembled with excitement. "What do we do now?"

"Go ahead and put on your gloves." Blaine pulled on a pair of latex gloves while Lily did the same. "Look, she's starting to stand."

"Should we make her lie down?"

"No, she knows what to do."

He held his breath as he watched for signs of a puppy… and there it was. The first little dog came out.

"It's a blue merle," he said. "Just like his mama."

Lily's eyes glistened with wonder as she brought her hands into the prayer position beneath her chin. "Wow, she did it. What do we do now?"

"We let her and the puppy bond and then we'll move the little guy to the side. Can you make sure the heating pad is warm underneath the blanket?"

Lily placed her palm in the corner of the whelping box. "It's on."

"Good. Do you want to give Tiara some water while I log the puppy in the book? Or do you want to log it?"

"I'll log it." She stood and found the book and pen.

The puppy showed no signs of distress and was bonding with its mama. One down. Who knew how many more to go? Blaine smiled to himself. He hoped there would be plenty more.

Voices from the front hall drew his attention. Lily raced to the doorway and turned back to Blaine. "I'm going to tell them the first puppy is here." She shut the door gently behind her.

Smart girl. She'd remembered all of the instructions he'd been giving her about keeping the room warm and quiet.

Blaine stroked Tiara's head. Her tongue hung out as she lifted clear blue eyes up to Blaine while the puppy nursed. He offered her a drink of water from a cup, and she lapped it up before turning away.

The door opened a fraction. Sienna and Lily entered, followed by his dad.

"The first one arrived, huh?" His dad crouched near Tiara and nodded with a satisfied grin to Blaine. "Looks like I picked the right time to drop supper off. The puppy's cute."

"Yeah, a boy. Pretty colors, don't you think?" Blaine's chest swelled with pride.

"Sure is. It'll be fun to see what the rest will look like." Dad straightened. "Food's on the counter when you're ready. I'll let your mother know the puppies are finally coming."

"You don't want to stay?" Blaine remained kneeling, keeping an eye on Tiara.

"Nah, you've got plenty of help here." His father's eyes twinkled as he turned to Sienna and winked. "Don't you get any ideas, missy."

Sienna chuckled and rubbed her belly. "No worries there. I've got plenty of time before this one is due."

Dad exited the room, and Sienna claimed his spot. "He is cute, isn't he? So tiny."

"Where's Connor?" Blaine peered back. "Doesn't he want to see the puppy?"

"He said he'll keep Ollie in the living room." Lily scooted around Sienna to kneel once more. "I think it grosses him out."

Blaine's lips twitched but he kept a lid on his laugh out of respect for the kid. Tiara's ears flattened backward as she began to pant.

"Lily, would you lift the puppy and move him to the corner like we talked about? I think Tiara's getting close to delivering another pup."

"Me? I can move him?"

Blaine nodded. Using both hands, she lifted the puppy to her chest for the tenderest of hugs, then placed it on top of the soft blanket, where the heating pad was located.

"I'm going to check on Connor." Sienna waved to the door.

"If you wait a few minutes, you'll get to see puppy number two arrive." Blaine watched as she turned the door handle.

"Uh, that's alright."

"Aunt Sienna, be sure to close the door quietly on your way out. We have to keep it warm in here for Tiara, and a loud noise might freak her out." Lily sounded serious.

"Got it."

Blaine glanced back as she left. He was surprised she didn't want to stay.

After a quick knock, the door opened slightly and Sienna's face popped back in. "Do you guys want me to fix you plates of food? Connor and I are going to eat."

"I'm not hungry," Lily said. "I need to take care of the puppies."

"I'll grab a bite later." Blaine kept his gaze on Tiara. "If you and Connor want to watch television, the remote's on the coffee table. I have a bunch of DVDs in the media cabinet, too. Help yourselves."

"Thanks, Blaine."

"I think another one's coming." Lily craned her neck to see.

"What do you think she'll have this time?"

"It had better be a girl." Her voice was dead serious. Blaine chuckled.

In no time, another puppy appeared. He and Lily repeated their routine.

"You got your wish, Lily. It's a girl. A black tri, like her daddy."

"Yay, a girl." She was careful not to raise her voice, but the triumph rang through clearly. "Look at the little white cross on her forehead. She's so cute."

Blaine returned the dog to her mama, and Tiara licked her as lovingly as she had the boy. Lily logged the data and rushed out to tell Connor and Sienna about the new addition.

Over the next two hours, five more puppies were born. Dusk fell, and Blaine urged Lily to take a break to eat some supper, but she told him she couldn't leave the puppies. He knew the feeling. He wouldn't eat until they were all delivered.

"Do you think she's done?" Lily asked half an hour later.

"I don't think so." He had a gut feeling she had at least one more in her.

"How do you know?"

"She's still panting."

"Should I give her some more vanilla ice cream?"

"No, she's okay for now." They'd tried to give Tiara a calcium supplement after puppy number four, but the dog had turned her head away, so they'd given her a small scoop of vanilla ice cream to lick. She hadn't turned her head away from ice cream. Who would?

Lily continued to keep watch over the puppies in the corner of the box, and Blaine took the opportunity to stand up and stretch. It had been a long day, and he'd be staying in here to check on Tiara and the pups all night.

The door opened slightly. "Is it safe to come in?"

"Yes."

Sienna tiptoed over to check out the puppies. Lily gave her the breakdown of the litter—four boys, three girls. Of them, three were black tris and four were blue merles.

"Oh, look, Aunt Sienna, she's going to have another!" Lily pointed to the dog, whose ears had flattened.

"I'll leave you both to it." Sienna put her palms up as she backed away.

"Don't you want to stay and watch?" Lily sounded incredulous.

"That's okay. Come out and let me know what she has." The door closed again.

Sienna, skittish? The thought made him grin. Blaine had never pegged her as the squeamish type.

"How about you help her out this time?" Blaine said to Lily.

"Me?" Lily pointed to her chest. "Really? What if something goes wrong, though? I don't want to hurt her or the puppy."

"If something's wrong, I'll take over."

She inhaled deeply and nodded. "Okay."

Five minutes later, another boy was in Lily's hands. Tears glistened in her eyes as she set the puppy in front of Tiara. He made sure the new pup—the runt of the litter—was nursing, then looked at Lily. "You did great."

"Thanks, Blaine. Thank you for letting me be here." She paused to swallow, clearly choked up. "This has been the best day of my life."

It ranked up there for him, too.

"You're going to have even better days than this one. I'm glad you were here to help. I couldn't have done it without you."

The words were true. Yes, he could have delivered the puppies and logged their stats, but having Lily here had taken a big load off his shoulders. He'd have to keep that in mind when making decisions about continuing to breed Tiara and Ollie. Could he do it on his own after Sienna and the kids left?

Did he want to?

He didn't need to decide tonight. But he'd have to figure it out before summer ended.

All of this puppy birthing had exhausted her, and she hadn't even been in the room. Around ten o'clock that night, Sienna stifled a yawn from where she was sitting on the bed in the spare room with a good view of the whelping box. The eight puppies were so little and squirmy and cute.

After all of them were born, Connor had brought in Ollie to see Tiara for a few minutes. Her nephew had petted the pups while Ollie licked Tiara's ear, then Sienna had taken the dog so Connor could stay and enjoy the puppies for a while.

Now that Lily and Blaine had eaten supper and Tiara was enjoying some well-deserved sleep, Sienna was ready to take the kids back to the cabin and get some sleep herself.

"Well, guys, I hate to break up the party, but it's getting late."

"Aww, no fair." Lily's face couldn't have drooped any lower. "I want to stay here. What if something happens to the puppies?"

"Nothing will happen to them." Sienna had complete confidence in Blaine.

"I'll be right here all night." Blaine gestured to the bed, confirming her faith in him.

"But the tiny one can barely find room to nurse. Look, all the other dogs are pushing him out of the way." Lily pointed to the smallest black tri, the one she'd delivered, whose little cries woke Tiara and had her nosing the pup back into the huddle of warm bodies.

"Her mama is taking care of it." Sienna put her hand on Lily's shoulder. She didn't want to rip the girl from the excitement, but they all needed to rest.

Talking to Blaine this morning about Connor felt like a lifetime ago. And then Troy had chosen that moment to text her when she hadn't heard from him in weeks. His text still had her stomach unsettled.

I miss you. I'm coming over to talk.

He missed her? Now? After all the awful things he'd said? After moving in with a woman old enough to be his mother? After telling her he never wanted to see the baby? That he didn't even want to know if it was a boy or a girl?

She didn't think so.

She'd texted him back that they could schedule a telephone call if he wanted. He hadn't responded.

"I won't be able to sleep." Lily trailed her finger down the tiny puppy's back. "I'll worry. I want to be here."

Blaine rubbed his chin. The bags under his eyes reminded her it had been a long day for him, too. He'd been so patient with her niece, so calm as the puppies were born—he had the kind of inner strength she admired in a man.

And Sienna couldn't help thinking how reassuring it would be to have a caring husband by her side when she had her own baby. That's why she'd passed on the opportunity to watch Tiara have her pups. Maybe it made it all too real—a reminder she wouldn't have a husband on hand to help with her child's birth.

She really did need to get some sleep.

"You guys can stay here if you want." Blaine's blue eyes shimmered as they met hers. "If we push the ottoman against the sectional, the kids can crash on it. And I have another guest room you could take."

Lily's face brightened with hope, and Sienna could sense the *please, please, please* about to erupt from her.

"I think we should head back to the cabin."

"I understand." Blaine stood, stretching his arms behind his back.

Sienna stared a beat too long at the chest muscles straining under his T-shirt, then pivoted and left the room, hurrying down the hall to the living room.

"We'd better go back, Connor." She noted how comfortable he looked with his ankles crossed on the chaise and Ollie's head on his lap.

"Can I finish the movie?" Connor asked. "I want to find out what happens."

Her nephew rarely asked for anything. Lily, on the other hand, wasn't afraid to speak up about something important to her.

Blaine entered the living room with a grin. "Come on, he's got to finish the movie."

Connor blinked a hopeful glance her way. She twisted her lips as she considered. As tired as she was, she was willing to compromise.

"Okay. But as soon as it's finished, we're heading back."

"Yes." Connor pumped his fist.

"Thanks, Aunt Sienna!" Lily called from the spare room.

"You okay in there for a little while, Lily?" Blaine asked.

"Yeah!"

"Holler if you need me. I'm going to relax out here for a minute."

"I will."

Blaine pushed the enormous ottoman against the sectional and sprawled out, letting his head fall back against the cushions. Sienna sat on an oversize chair adjacent to him. It, too, had an ottoman, and the instant her legs were propped up, she felt better.

"What happens now that the puppies are born?" she asked.

Blaine lifted his head. "I'll be here with them constantly for the next couple of days. Next week, Dad offered to puppysit in the mornings so I can get some work done. I'll be on puppy duty in the afternoons. Jim, Bryce and Connor, here, offered to deal with the bulk of the chores."

The way he said it made her think he'd prefer to be out on the ranch rather than here with the dogs.

"These puppies are cramping your style, aren't they?" she teased.

"Nah." His lips curved up. "The first week is the hardest. It's just… I have a lot of stuff going on with one of my pastures."

Connor glanced at them as he continued to stroke Ollie's back. "We've been checking it every day to figure out when to cut it for hay."

She was glad her nephew was contributing to the conversation. He seemed excited about checking a pasture. Go figure.

"Yeah, I really wanted to get out there." Blaine's face fell. "It will be a few days before I can check it again."

"Won't one of the cowboys check it for you?" she asked.

"He's got to see if it's growing right." Connor had resumed watching the movie and kept his gaze glued to the television.

"Can it grow wrong?" she asked.

"It's not growing at all." Blaine looked every bit as exhausted as she felt. "Well, that's not true. It's just the lack of rain. I'd hoped the grain would be taller and the pasture thicker by now. And time's running out."

"Oh, I see." She had no clue what pastures were supposed to look like. She did understand rain, though, and it had been weeks since they'd had any. "If it rains soon, will that help?"

He sighed, shrugging. "I want it to, but this late in the game? I have a feeling the pasture is as full as it's going to get this year. I can only hope it, along with the other pastures I cut for hay, will be enough to help feed the cattle all winter."

Another thing Sienna knew next to nothing about. "Is that all they eat? Hay?"

"I have a lot of acreage for them to graze. We move them around all winter, but the forage isn't enough, especially when it comes time for calving. So I feed them hay, too."

"The ranch keeps you busy." And here she thought her life was jam-packed.

"You don't know the half of it, Aunt Sienna," Connor said. "He takes care of the steers and rides out to make sure none of the cattle are sick. Yesterday, Jim roped a cow and gave him a shot of medicine because its hoof had something wrong with it. It was cool."

Blaine shot her a surprised look that said *a rotten hoof is cool?* She suppressed a laugh.

Connor glanced at Blaine, then Sienna. "We should take Lily around on the four-wheelers so she can see the cows and the new pasture."

Sienna blinked, realizing Blaine was right. Getting on a four-wheeler to ride out under a summer sky was Connor's idea of fun, just like it had been Blaine's and hers at that age.

Blaine held her gaze, and something stirred in her—the feeling of being young and free again.

She turned her attention to her hands resting on her lap. "You'd have to drag your sister away from the puppies first."

"No problem." Connor grinned. "We'll be here for weeks."

That they would. But would she be able to squash these feelings for Blaine?

Stay focused on the kids. It was what she did best.

Chapter Five

Dry as a bone. Just as he'd feared.

Blaine crouched on a bare patch in the dead pasture Monday morning. This was the first time he'd been able to get away from the puppies to check on the land. On Saturday, he'd taken them and Tiara to the veterinarian, and they'd all been deemed to be fine. By last night, he'd been exhausted from making sure Tiara had enough to eat and that all of the pups were still nursing properly and gaining weight. Even with Lily's help, the past few days had been a lot of work.

He was thankful to have a break from the puppies, even though they sure were cute. They were in capable hands with Lily and Dad. When Blaine mentioned needing to find them homes once they were weaned, Lily hadn't liked the idea at all. That's how life worked, though.

Sometimes siblings went their separate ways, and there was nothing you could do to change it.

Blaine rose, twirling a long stalk of wheatgrass between his thumb and finger. It wasn't brittle...yet. He'd have to keep a close eye on the pasture. If he waited too long, it would become brittle and difficult to cut and bale. If he cut it too early, the nutrients in the grass might be stunted.

The stalk bent between his fingers. It still had too much give in it, but it wouldn't for long. If the weather got hot and the moisture stayed low, he'd have to consider cutting the wheatgrass earlier than he'd originally planned.

Boots was nibbling on the grass, and Blaine took a moment to stroke the horse's neck before hoisting himself back in the saddle. He wasn't in a rush to return to real life. Four days of being cooped up inside without the sky above him had taken their toll.

His mental to-do list started ticking through his brain. Jim had fixed the damaged fence. The bulls were getting rowdier, a sure sign that mating season would be here soon. He'd kept several steers last fall, and they'd been behaving themselves for the time being. He doubted the good behavior would last, though.

He signaled for Boots to head toward the ridge farther out. The gully beyond it tended to hold a few inches of water even in the driest conditions. He hoped it still did.

As the ridge came into view, he added planning something fun for the kids to his list. There hadn't been time for him and Sienna to work out anything since they'd discussed it.

His phone rang, and he slipped it out of his pocket, answering the call without looking at it.

"Hello?" He hoped nothing was wrong with the puppies.

"We're getting together Friday night. It's been way too long." His best friend, Randy Watkins, was on the line, and Blaine grinned.

"Agreed. What are we looking at?" He kept an eye out for the gulley as Boots picked his way across the rockier terrain.

"Hannah's calling the girls. I offered up my grill and the backyard, but she said we're all heading to Mac's for barbecue and a bonfire."

His good mood faltered. Up until recently, when one of the guys called to get together it meant just the guys. No women. But his friends had all been pairing up, getting engaged, getting married, even starting families.

It was enough to make a single guy like him want to hurl.

"What should I bring?" He knew he sounded like he'd been sentenced to prison rather than invited on a fun outing, but he couldn't help it.

"Bring Sienna and the kids. Bridget and Tess insist."

Another thing that annoyed him—everyone seemed to know what was going on way before he did.

"I'll ask them." But they might not want to come. Hanging out with a bunch of adults wouldn't be fun for a couple of teenagers.

"I guess Kaylee's having a few friends over, too, so they'll get to meet some other teens."

Had every argument he hadn't even mentioned been taken care of?

The women were behind this.

And it wasn't only Mac's fiancée, Bridget—who, he admitted, wasn't really the meddling type. It was the wives. Tess, who *was* the meddling type and married to his friend Sawyer Roth. And Holly, Jet's wife, who made no secret she was in matchmaking mode. Not to mention Hannah, Randy's fiancé, who taught elementary school in town and had weddings on her mind, since she and Randy had set the date for the first week in August. Mac and Bridget were getting married in September.

Which left him and Austin Watkins, Randy's brother, to hold the line and stay single. Although, now that Austin had a one-year-old son, Blaine wasn't sure how long he'd last as a bachelor, either.

"You still there?" Randy asked.

"Yeah, I'm here."

"Alright. I'll see you Friday at Mac's. Six thirty."

"Got it." He ended the call as the gully came into view. After dismounting, he bent to study the water level.

It couldn't be more than an inch deep.

This wasn't good. They needed rain more than ever.

Maybe a Friday night barbecue at Mac's would be a good thing after all. He could pick the guys' brains about the water levels at their ranches. Find out when they planned on cutting hay.

And if Sienna did come, his friends would be a much-needed buffer. Every time he got near her, he'd catch a trace of her tropical perfume or start staring at all that luxurious hair.

He'd forget she was leaving.

He'd forget she was pregnant.

He'd forget she was off-limits.

He needed to remember all of the above before he got hurt.

"The puppies will be in good hands, I promise." Sienna checked her makeup in the cabin's bathroom Friday while Lily continued insisting she didn't want to go to some stranger's house. "Kevin and Julie will keep them out of trouble."

"Will they even notice if little Sushi gets a chance to eat? Those other puppies bully him."

Sienna swiped on lip gloss and puckered her lips, blowing herself a kiss in the mirror. She'd had the same argument with Lily for five days running. The girl didn't want to go to Mac's. She wanted to stay here with the puppies.

But she'd spent almost every waking hour with them already. Sienna had practically dragged her to the candle shop every afternoon, and only when Lily would see Clara toddle up to her with her chubby arms in the air would she snap out of her puppy obsession.

What on earth was Sienna going to do at the end of July, when Lily would have to leave the puppies permanently? A shiver rippled down her back. She wouldn't think about it now.

"Sushi is gaining weight like the rest of them. He'll be as big as Otto soon."

"None of them will ever be as big as Otto."

Lily had given each puppy a nickname, and it had been fun watching them get bigger, although none of them were able to do much beyond eating, sleeping and letting out little cries when they'd strayed a few inches from their mama at this point.

Sienna exited the bathroom as Connor brushed past her to check his hair. She smiled to herself. He looked cute and a little nervous. He'd been told by Bryce that there would be girls his age at Mac's place. She hoped he'd hit it off with the other teenagers.

"Come on, Lily, get ready. Blaine's picking us up soon." Sienna paused in the doorway to her room. Her hair needed combing, but the shorts and pink T-shirt were fine for the evening.

She could hear Connor's voice coming from the bathroom, so Sienna leaned back. Was he calling her? She kept her ears open.

And wished she hadn't.

"I can't talk now, Mom… I know, I'm sorry you're upset…"

She clenched her jaw.

Becca would not ruin this night for him.

She strode briskly to him. "Let me talk to your mother." She held out her hand.

He gave her a guilty look, and that bothered her, too. He had no reason to feel guilty.

"Aunt Sienna wants to talk to you."

She could hear Becca's sniffles as he passed her his phone. She flashed him an understanding smile and took the phone to the living room.

"We're headed to a barbecue," Sienna said. "What's going on?"

"I miss the kids. Put Connor back on." The sound of her blowing her nose made her sigh.

"Is it Aaron?"

"You know it is." There was an edge to her voice.

"Why don't you tell me about it?"

"I don't want to bother you. Put Connor back on."

"He's busy." She held her breath, waiting for the outburst.

"Too busy to talk to his mother?" Becca's voice rose.

Sienna counted to three. "Yes, we're leaving soon. Listen, why don't you get out tonight? It's beautiful weather. It's the weekend. Call Aaron. Invite him over."

"He wouldn't want to come…" Her voice faded.

"How do you know?"

"He's been distant. Couples' therapy didn't go well yesterday."

In that case, Sienna was surprised Becca had waited this long to call Connor.

"I'm sorry, Bec. I am. I know you guys are trying. Just hang in there."

"Yeah, well, it's hard. He knows he's abandoning me. And he doesn't care."

The knock on the front door could only be Blaine. Sienna had to wrap this up. "I've got to go. Want me to call you when I get home?"

Lily trudged to the door and ushered Blaine inside. Sienna held up her index finger to him, indicating she was almost finished.

"Don't bother. I'll be fine…" Becca's voice trailed off to prove she would *not* be fine.

"I'll call you later."

"Whatever."

Sienna ended the call as Connor emerged from the bathroom.

"Is everything alright?" Blaine frowned at her. She handed Connor his phone back.

"Yes. Give Lily a minute to brush her hair, and we'll be ready."

Lily glared at her and practically stomped to the bathroom.

"What's wrong with her?" Blaine asked.

"She doesn't want to leave the puppies," Connor replied.

Sienna picked up the plate of lemon bars she'd baked this morning. The less she talked right now, the better. A minute later, with her hair tamed, Lily marched past the three of them and stormed out the front door.

"Shall we?" Sienna gave Blaine a tight smile.

What was supposed to be a fun night out was turning out to be stressful and tense. *Lord, can't anything just be easy for once?* She could only hope the night would get better. Friday nights were supposed to be fun.

Blaine watched Sienna laughing at something Bridget said, and his heart felt funny. Reagan would probably call it the pitter-patter of his heartbeat, but she was girlie like that. Whatever it was, he was positive it had everything to do with his attraction to Sienna and nothing to do with a possible arrhythmia.

Why couldn't he tear his eyes away from her? Pretty sundress, lightly tanned arms, big smile, sparkling green eyes—yep, she was the whole package. The ladies had insisted on having her sit in one of the Adirondack chairs while he and Mac got the fire going. From the pastel peaches and lavenders spreading out across the sky, he'd give it half an hour before the sun headed home for the night. The snap and crackle of dry logs burning mingled with the conversations.

The teens were all still in Mac's fancy pole barn, playing their version of *Would You Rather*. Blaine was glad he didn't have to take part in it. Kaylee had introduced Connor and Lily to the handful of friends—a mix of boys and girls—she'd invited. Connor seemed to be fitting in well, as much as he could tell. All in all, a successful evening as far as Sienna and the kids were concerned.

But for him?

He should have just skipped the whole thing.

He didn't need all these reminders that everyone's

lives were moving on while his stayed the same. At least the food had been good.

Austin dropped into the seat next to him with a grunt. "Hey, man, sorry we got interrupted earlier. Sidney's babysitting and wasn't sure if AJ could have Jell-O. Where she got Jell-O from, I have no clue. I don't buy the stuff." He shook his head. "So what's going on?"

Finally. Normal talk. Guy talk. Ranch talk.

Blaine shifted to face him. "Earlier I was out checking a gully in one of the pastures. I've never seen it this low before. If it had an inch of water in it, I'd be surprised."

"I know." Austin shook his head, blowing out a loud exhalation. "This dry spell has me worried. I know nobody wants to say the word *drought*, but…"

Blaine nodded as all the implications came back to him. "I'm getting nervous."

"The new pasture not taking? You planted wheatgrass, right? Having trouble with it?"

"It's not taking as well as I'd hoped."

"It is drought-resistant."

"Yeah, but it has to get established first. The pasture looks patchy."

Jet strolled their way, and Blaine clamped his mouth shut. He did not need any of his brother's I-told-you-so's right now.

Austin cracked his knuckles. "If it helps, I'm worried, too. Last year I debated if I should try to grow more hay as protection for the coming winter or just let the cattle graze the acres I was considering reseeding. Honestly, I'm trying to get a few more years out of my current equipment, so I opted for grazing. But there's barely anything for them to graze."

"The cold snap in May didn't help."

"The winds didn't, either." Austin stared at the fire. "I guess we can be thankful we didn't get hail. It could be worse."

"You should have told me about the equipment." Jet stood in front of them, his back to the flames. "You could have borrowed ours."

"I know, but I didn't want to," Austin said. "If anything breaks down on my watch…well, I don't want to be responsible."

"The offer stands. Anytime." Jet grabbed one of the camping chairs to sit next to them. "You're better off letting the cattle graze, anyhow. Blaine spent a big chunk of change on reseeding the dead pasture, and he couldn't have picked a worse time to do it."

Blaine stiffened as he gritted his teeth. His brother might as well announce to everyone that he was just a stupid bum who didn't have a clue how to run a ranch.

"It's hard to predict a drought." Austin shrugged. Blaine relaxed slightly. At least Austin got it. Jet acted like he had the inside scoop on everything to do with ranching and would never make a mistake.

Admittedly, his brother rarely made mistakes. But still.

Sawyer came over and sat next to Austin, angling his chair toward them.

"I thought I heard the word *drought*." Sawyer's lips drew together in a tight line. "We could really use rain."

Randy strolled over with Ned, the service dog for his heart condition, and sat, too. Mac wasn't far behind.

"I don't think I'll be able to cut even three quarters of the hay I put up last year." Mac toyed with a soda can in his hand.

"The creek behind my house is low." Randy puffed his cheeks. "The fishing is getting bad. Higher temps. Less oxygen. More predators picking them off. I don't like it."

All six of them stayed silent as ripples of female laughter on the other side of the fire reached them.

"Are you guys at a funeral or what?" Tess yelled, getting to her feet. "Mac, why don't you put some music on. This is a bonfire, not a wake."

"That's my lady." Sawyer rolled his eyes, grinning.

"What are you in the mood for?" Mac called back, rising out of his chair.

"Something lively."

"I'll help." Randy got up, joining Mac as he headed inside the pole barn, where a sound system had been installed. Speakers were mounted near the concrete patio area and strings of bare bulbs dangled overhead. They were attached to a pergola full of climbing flowers.

Holly drifted over to stand next to Jet. He wrapped his arm around her waist and drew her onto his lap. Blaine was used to their affection, but it was still hard to take sometimes. He glanced Sienna's way. She was nodding at something Bridget said.

"I've been a little worried about Reagan lately," Holly said. Blaine peered her way, thinking she was talking to Jet, but she was addressing him. "I think she misses Erica."

"She should go visit her," Blaine said. "Stay a week or two."

"Your mom and I have mentioned it, but she blows us off."

"Want me to talk to her?" Jet asked.

"No." She gave Jet a tender smile then turned to Blaine. "Actually, I was hoping, Blaine, that you'd convince her to go to the rodeo next Friday. Mac and Bridget are taking Kaylee. They invited Sienna and Connor and Lily. If they're all going, maybe you could bring Reagan. She needs to get out."

Mac and Bridget had asked Sienna to the rodeo? He'd thought *he* was going to take her and the kids.

Holly was staring at him with her big blue eyes, the ones that saw too much. Admittedly, if they saw too much with him, they likely saw too much with his sister, too.

Holly was right. For the past year, Reagan had been going out less—and she'd never been one to get out much even before Erica got married.

"I'll take her to the rodeo." His mind flipped through to check if he'd missed more warning signs with Reagan. He couldn't think of anything offhand. "Do you think there's more to it?"

"What do you mean?" Holly asked.

"With Reagan."

"I don't know. I hope not. I wish she'd put herself out there a little. Go on a few dates."

Blaine couldn't think of anyone Reagan would want to date. Frankly, he couldn't think of anyone *he'd* want to date his little sister.

"I'll get her to the rodeo." Blaine threw up his hands. "As for dating, that's on you. I'm not rustling up a cowboy for her."

"I'm not, either." Jet shared a knowing look with him, then frowned at Holly. "Reagan doesn't need a guy to make her happy."

"Yeah, she's got the candles." Blaine gave a firm nod. "She loves making them."

"No one said she doesn't enjoy making the candles."

Holly stood again. "But she deserves to have someone to love, too."

He supposed he should be happy Holly wasn't trying to set *him* up with anyone. His gaze strayed to Sienna. Her head tilted as their eyes met. A rush of heat warmed his body. Only a fool would get attached to a pregnant woman who'd be leaving soon.

Unlike his friends, he'd never fallen in love. But the woman staring back at him had sure grabbed his attention.

Chapter Six

"It can't wait any longer." The following Tuesday morning, Blaine slid open the barn door where he kept the farm equipment. "We've got to start cutting the hay today."

Jim smoothed his mustache and headed straight to the tractor. "The extra blades arrived if one of them breaks."

He and Jim had spent time over the weekend greasing and tightening bolts on all the equipment. They'd both agreed if the weather stayed dry and warm, they'd best get the prairie grass cut soon, even if it was a week earlier than they'd hoped.

"*If* one of them breaks?" Blaine tossed Jim the keys to the all-purpose tractor. "I'd be shocked if we don't have to replace at least three when it's all said and done."

"I reckon you're right." He adjusted his cowboy hat as he chuckled. "While you're cutting, I'll brief Bryce and Connor on the cattle grazing the southeast pasture. They can check the cows on my radar out there. I'll take care of the rest of the herd. I'll hook up the rake now, and when I'm finished checking cattle, I'll start combing the windrows together so you can get to baling."

"Good plan. It will give me a chance to get a head start on cutting. With the grass so sparse this year, we might have to combine two or three windrows together."

"I was thinking the same. It'll be too hard to bale if we don't. It's a shame."

It really was a shame. Blaine wished they'd gotten rain in May when they'd needed it. Early June still would have made a difference. But they hadn't had a drop since late April. He supposed he should take Austin's lead and be thankful hail hadn't destroyed the pastures. Grasshoppers could do a number on them, too.

Lord, forgive me for not seeing the blessings even in the troubles. This could be worse.

He and Jim discussed the order of the fields they planned on cutting, and then Blaine climbed into the swather and drove it into the sunshine.

Connor and Bryce had both offered to help out more while he and Jim were haying, and Blaine was thankful to have two hardworking ranch hands available. It saved him time and allowed him to concentrate solely on getting the hay in.

As he drove the swather down the dirt lane, his mind wandered here and there, stopping on Sienna. As usual.

Friday night on the way back home from Mac's, Connor and Lily had seemed excited when Sienna mentioned the rodeo. They'd had a good time meeting Kaylee and her friends. Blaine had asked Sienna if she and the kids wanted to ride with him, and she'd laughed and said, "Of course," which had eased his mind about Mac and Bridget setting up the rodeo excursion.

He'd even gotten Reagan on board. On Saturday afternoon, he'd taken his sister to Bridget's coffee shop and asked her to come to the rodeo with them. At first, she'd declined, but he'd told her he really wanted her to come. She'd finally nodded and agreed. They'd chatted a bit, and he'd been surprised when she admitted how much she missed Erica and how making the candles wasn't the same without her around.

Holly was obviously on to something there, but he had no clue how to fix it. He'd just listened and nodded. He wished he'd had some advice to give, but he didn't, so he'd let her talk. Jet surely would have known the right thing to say.

Oh, well. Blaine couldn't change his personality.

The grass on either side of the lane swayed in the wind. It was still flexible, ripe for cutting. He'd be mowing those fields later this week. For now, he was starting at the one farthest away—Grandpa's dead pasture. An eagle flew overhead in the distance, reminding him how blessed he was to own this peaceful, quiet land.

As he neared the dead pasture, his chest tightened. How many hay bales would they end up with from it? How many would they get out of the other fields?

There wasn't anything he could do to control the situation, so he forced his mind elsewhere. The puppies were doing well. Lily had begged Sienna to stay with them in the afternoons instead of watching Clara at the candle shop, and they'd compromised. She could stay with the puppies in the mornings while his dad was there, but she had to go to the candle shop with Sienna after lunch.

Blaine had to give it to his father—the man not only offered to puppysit so Blaine could continue working, but he also showed up every morning with sacks of groceries so he could make the big suppers everyone on the ranch enjoyed. He'd put a video baby monitor in the spare room to keep an eye on the pups while he cooked. Pretty smart.

When the pasture came into view, Blaine turned the swather toward the far end. His nerves sizzled and frayed.

Lord, this is all I've got. I'm not a take-charge guy, like Jet. I don't have Reagan's creative side. I certainly don't have Erica's social skills. But I love the land You gave me. Please let the hay be enough this year.

A part of him wanted Jet to see that he made good decisions, too, and that he deserved his half of the ranch. But the other part of him felt it was stupid, really, to crave his brother's approval.

Turning the swather to the very edge of the field, he hesitated before dropping the blades.

The knee-high grass seemed to wave like the sea, but he knew if he climbed down now and looked at it close up, it would be thin on the ground.

Blaine took a deep breath and steered the machine forward.

Here goes nothing.

"Time to go." Sienna stood in the doorway to Blaine's spare room, watching Lily hold two squirming puppies. Kevin had brought in a dining room chair at some point and was reading the newspaper. She had a feeling that from here on out, she'd be arguing with Lily about going to the candle shop every weekday afternoon. Her niece was obsessed with the puppies.

"Aww, do I have to?" Lily's big hazel eyes pleaded with her. "Look, Aunt Sienna, all of the puppies except Sushi can actually get up on all fours now. What if he can't walk like the rest of them?"

Kevin looked over the paper. "Sushi will be walking within a day, Lil. Don't worry about him."

"But how do you know?"

He gave her an indulgent smile. "I grew up on this ranch. Been watching animals my whole life. When you have as much experience as I do, you just know about these things."

Lily narrowed her eyes in a skeptical glance.

"Tell you what." He folded the paper and set it on his lap. "I'll text you the instant he can hold his weight on those front legs. I'll even video it. Deal?"

Her lips twitched in disappointment, but finally she nodded. "Deal."

"Off you go." He waved to them with a smile. "The puppies will be here when you get back."

Sienna moved aside for Lily to leave ahead of her. "Do you need anything from the cabin before we head over?"

"No."

Outside, Lily stomped to Sienna's vehicle and got into the passenger seat, jerking her seat belt over her lap and buckling it with an attitude.

Sienna was never sure how to handle these situations. Should she lecture Lily about not taking her disappointment out on her? Or should she ignore it, chalking it up to normal thirteen-year-old behavior?

She got in, started the car and headed to the candle shop. Given the fact Lily was living in a new place while her parents' marriage was still in limbo, Sienna was willing to give her some grace. Plus, she'd been very helpful not just with the puppies, but with Clara, too. A lecture wouldn't be appropriate.

The baby had been active in her tummy ever since lunch, and she thought of the upcoming prenatal appointment she'd scheduled with the local family practice in Sunrise Bend. *Someday, about thirteen years from now, you and I might be having this same type of car ride.*

*You'll be all mad at me for dragging you away from
something fun, and I'll be wondering if I should say
something about it then, too.*

She smiled as the prairie rolled by. Off in the distance she could see a couple of riders on horseback approaching a herd of cattle. Probably Connor and Bryce.
Her nephew had been in great spirits ever since Friday
night. He'd hit it off with Kaylee's friends, especially her
best friend, Lydia. And when Blaine and Jim had asked
him to help out extra hours this week, he'd jumped at
the chance.

She couldn't have asked for a better experience here
when it came to him. She loved seeing him blossom,
and it helped that Becca had been in a good mood for
the past few days as well. When Sienna called her after
the bonfire Friday night, Becca hadn't wanted to talk
because Aaron had showed up with a pizza. What a relief that had been.

Maybe her sister and Aaron really would work things
out. And Connor and Lily could have their family back
together before school started in the fall. Wouldn't that
be something?

Sienna parked in front of the candle shop and turned
to Lily, who was still wearing an icy expression.

"You ready?" She gave her niece a smile.

The girl grunted.

She hoped Lily wouldn't be like this in front of the
Mayer women. It would be embarrassing. Maybe she
should say something about being rude…

Lily was already out the door and halfway to the shop
by the time Sienna figured out what she wanted to say.
She sighed. If Lily continued to be disrespectful, she'd
speak to her then.

Her phone rang and, recognizing her divorce attorney's number, she answered it. "Hello?"

"How are you, Sienna? Is this a good time?"

Her blood froze in her veins. She tried to prepare herself for the words she didn't want to hear.

"I'm fine, and, yes, I can talk now."

"I just got off the phone with Troy's attorney. They've drafted a petition to terminate his parental rights as soon as the baby is born."

"Can he legally do that?" She hadn't researched it. She'd been too afraid of what she'd find out.

"In some circumstances, yes. Usually, the other parent files the petition and the court decides. When a parent tries to voluntarily waive their rights, it's more difficult."

A feather of relief eased her tension.

"Troy's case is unusual, though, because he's attached a doctor's diagnosis of a borderline personality disorder. Given the mental-illness angle, there is a good chance the court will decide in his favor."

She'd been right all along. Troy had a personality disorder.

Inhaling sharply, she didn't know what to think. Didn't know what to feel.

The few times she'd brought up the possibility to Troy, he'd coldly shut her down, implying she was a monster for even suggesting it.

He must really hate her and the baby to go to these lengths.

"My question is would you support this? It would help his case if you want his parental rights taken away, too. If you're worried about the baby's safety at all, this is the time to make a decision."

She wanted to end the call and toss the phone as far away as possible. Instead, she steadied herself by placing her hand on the hood of the vehicle.

"I don't know. I don't think he'd ever physically harm our baby." But emotionally?

"It's a lot to take in. I'll email you the documents his lawyer gave me. Look them over. Think about what's best for you and the baby. I'm here if you have any questions."

"Thank you. I will."

She expected him to say goodbye, but he paused. "Do you think he's doing this to get out of paying child support?"

"No." She thrust her fingers through her hair. "I mean, yeah, he doesn't want to pay child support, but it's deeper than that."

"If this is going to hurt you financially, we can fight it." The sound of paper rustling came through the line. "When you've made a decision, let me know what you want to do."

"Wait." Her thick brain was starting to loosen up. "If I agree I don't want him having parental rights, is that the end of it?"

"No. There would still be a court date and a hearing."

"And if I do nothing?"

"It will be up to him to prove he should be allowed no rights."

She asked a few more questions before they ended the call. As she stared at the phone in her hand, a hollowness spread in her chest.

Troy really did have a mental-health issue. She hadn't been imagining it.

But would he harm their child?

She couldn't imagine him being violent. He'd never

laid a hand on her. But his wild mood swings, his unpredictability, his manipulative words—they'd taken a toll on her. She'd never known what she was getting on the few weekends each month he was in town. It would be asking a lot from a child to understand it, too.

Maybe it would be easier this way.

Sienna forced her feet forward. She wouldn't have to deal with him or worry he'd confuse their child with his extreme mood swings and odd decision-making. He was bound to let down their child.

Was *easy* the best solution, though?

Inside the showroom, Sienna paused to get her bearings. Lily was beaming and holding Clara on her hip.

"And how are you today?" Lily tweaked Clara's nose. The toddler giggled. "Are we going to bake some cake?" She set her on her feet and took her by the hand over to the play kitchen near Holly's desk.

At least Lily had gotten into a good mood.

"Sienna." Julie peeked her head through the door leading to the workshop area. "I'm trying a new scent. Want to learn how to make it?"

"I'd love to." Anything to take her mind off her ex.

She hurried to the back and soaked in the workshop. Julie and Reagan made all the candles back here. Sienna enjoyed putting the orders together with their careful packaging method. Crinkled strips of heavy paper in various colors nestled the products in special boxes with dividers. It satisfied the precision-oriented part of her, the one that dotted every *i* and crossed every *t* when preparing the grants for the college.

Ever since arriving, she'd been hoping to actually learn how to make the candles, too. It looked like today was her chance. Something good to follow something bad.

The workshop held rows of metal industrial shelving and carefully planned workspaces, wax melters and supplies. It was a far cry from her office at the college. A laptop, file organizer and stacks of manila folders took up most of her desk there. She did have a window with a nice view of the campus, though.

"Have a seat. Are you feeling okay? How's the baby?" Julie patted the stool next to her. Sienna realized they were alone.

"Where's Reagan?"

"She's taking a long lunch. Meeting Hannah to go over bridesmaid things for the wedding."

"That sounds fun." Sienna liked Reagan. Was drawn to her, really. Blaine's sister had a gentle spirit.

"I hope so." Her eyebrows drew together. "I don't know about her lately. I hope being in this wedding sparks her to get out more."

"Well, she's going to the rodeo with me and Blaine and his friends on Friday."

"Is she?" Julie perked up. "She didn't tell me."

"Yes, and Kaylee's friends are coming, too. They promised to show Connor and Lily the best food trucks." Sienna rubbed her baby bump as Julie got up and took various items off the shelf behind them.

"Do me a favor." She set wax melts and two fragrance tubes on the worktable. "If you see a cute cowboy, get his number for her."

Sienna snorted out a laugh. Blaine's mom sat back down and thumbed through a binder until coming to the page marked *Soy*.

"Reagan and I used to wing it when we first started making candles, but we could never quite capture the exact scent twice. She insisted we write every measurement down, along with detailed instructions."

"Like a cookbook." Sienna leaned over to read the page. It was full of measurements in columns and rows for various scents and sizes of the candles. She had to admit, she was impressed that Reagan had put all these detailed charts together.

"Exactly." Julie walked her through the process, and while they made a batch, Sienna's mind drifted to Troy only a few times.

"Now we let them cool." Julie began tidying the workspace.

"And tomorrow I'll be packaging them and sending them out."

"Some of them." Her eyes twinkled. "The rest will get stored for future orders. And Reagan will keep coming up with new scent combinations. That girl can't turn it off. Sometimes I shake my head and think there's no way it will smell good, but she usually makes winners. She's talented."

"And creative." Sienna glanced Julie's way and gave her a smile. "But so are you."

"Aww, thanks. I do love making candles. I think a big part of it is being here with you girls. Keeps me young."

Sienna's phone chimed and she checked it. Lily had texted Can you come out here?

"Uh-oh. Lily needs me. I hope nothing's wrong." Sienna stood and returned to the showroom, where she zoomed over to Lily. "What's going on?"

"Sushi's walking! Mr. Mayer sent me a video. You have to see it!" Lily sidled up next to Sienna. A video of the puppies began playing. Their little cries were too cute. And then the camera panned to Sushi, who, sure enough, pushed himself to stand and hobbled a few steps before collapsing.

"Can we go back? I want to see it for myself."

"I'm afraid not." Sienna hated letting her down. "We have work to do, but we can stop by as soon as we finish up here."

Lily crossed her arms over her chest, her face in a pout. "Mom would let me."

Sienna was taken aback. It wasn't like Lily to compare her to her mom.

"Your mom's not here, and I am. We made a commitment to work here in the afternoons. And we honor our commitments. The Mayers have been very generous to allow us to stay with them. We don't even have to cook our suppers, because Mr. Mayer does it for us. Helping out with the candles is the least we can do." She normally wouldn't be this stern with Lily, but the combination of the girl's earlier attitude combined with the phone call about Troy must have short-circuited her patience.

"I don't want to help with the candles. I want to help with the puppies."

"Lily—"

"Never mind." She spun on her heel and stalked over to the corner, where two accent chairs flanked a small table. Staring at her phone, she slumped in one of the chairs.

That went well.

Sienna tried to calm her frayed nerves. For the first time she could remember, she resented the position she was in. Disciplining Lily was Becca's job. And this whole parental-rights thing was what Troy wanted, not her. Why did she have to make all the tough decisions?

God, I'm having a hard time here. I don't think I'm strong enough. And I don't know if I want to be anymore.

The sun was lower in the sky than he anticipated when he called it quits for the day. Blaine surveyed the dead pasture with its giant rolls of baled hay. He'd managed to mow the entire thing at a whopping six miles per hour while only breaking one of the swather's blades. He would have preferred breaking none of them, but hey, after climbing under and into the cutter head, he'd only lost a minor chunk of skin on his pinkie while replacing the blade. Not bad, all things considered.

Jim had shown up this afternoon on the tractor pulling the rake. While Jim combined the rows of mowed grass—it had been sparse enough to combine three rows at a time—Blaine had driven to one of his primary hay pastures and cut the grass there. Then he'd returned to the dead pasture with the baler.

"Stupid rocks." He kicked at the parched dirt now fully visible without the tall grass hiding it. One of the stones had clogged the baler earlier, and he'd wasted precious time unwedging it. He supposed he should be glad it hadn't bent any of the teeth.

The harvest could have been better. How many times over the past nine months had he dreamed about seeing roll after roll of prime hay in this pasture?

There might not be as many rolls as he wanted, but what was there was good. It would help feed the herd all winter.

Blaine took off his cowboy hat and wiped his brow with a handkerchief. If the rest of the week was forecasted to be this hot, he'd better get the remaining hay cut ASAP. He couldn't afford it drying out and getting too brittle to mow. He needed every single one of those bales.

It was going to be a long, hard week. And if he didn't get all the hay in by Friday afternoon, he might have to skip the rodeo. This land was too important.

Sienna would still enjoy herself. She'd be with his friends. She'd have Connor and Lily and Reagan.

You were the one who suggested giving the kids a fun summer. The rodeo's part of it.

So what? They didn't need him to have a good time.

And Reagan won't go if you don't take her. You're really going to let her down, too?

At the sour taste in his mouth, he shifted his jaw and stared off in the distance. A small herd of pronghorn was grazing. Beautiful, graceful creatures. He always loved to see them take off and run.

Isn't that what you're doing? Running from your responsibility?

No, the ranch was his responsibility. Everything else came second.

He could practically hear his mom's voice: *People are more important than cows, dear.* How many times had she said that to their father over the years? Too many to count.

Slapping the hat back on his head, he climbed into the baler and started it up. As he drove to the ranch, he wrestled with his priorities.

Maybe he was worrying for nothing. He might be able to finish haying by Friday.

Come on, you know waiting until Monday won't make that big of a difference.

Was this about the hay or being with Sienna? Why was he so worked up about going to the rodeo, anyhow?

It wasn't a big deal. He'd been to a million of them. He'd buy too much greasy food, share some laughs with his friends and call it a night.

But this time it wouldn't only be his friends. It would be their wives, their girlfriends. It would be all the teens. And his sister. And Sienna.

Life was easier when it was just him and the guys.

Chapter Seven

A thrill rippled through Sienna as she climbed out of Blaine's truck Friday night in the parking lot. She joined him, Reagan and Connor at the back of the truck. Lily had begged to stay home with the puppies, and since Julie and Kevin would be there, Sienna had reluctantly agreed. Personally, she wanted Lily to get out and enjoy what summer had to offer, but it had been one argument after another all week, and she was plain worn out from working around Lily's obsession with the pups.

Ever since the bonfire at Mac's, Sienna had been looking forward to tonight to spend more time with all of Blaine's supportive friends. They helped take her mind off the other stuff going on—Becca's ups and downs, Troy's diagnosis, the conversation with her lawyer and the fact she was having a baby soon and wasn't remotely prepared for it. Which reminded her, she needed to call Erica tomorrow to find out how her doctor's appointment had gone this afternoon. They talked every few days and texted more often.

"Hey, Connor!"

Sienna turned to see who was calling her nephew.

His cheeks were flushed as he waved to Kaylee and her friend Lydia. A few other teens were joking around behind them.

"Is it okay if I go with them, Aunt Sienna?"

"Of course. Have fun. Oh, wait—" She fished in her small cross-body purse for her wallet. "I've got some money for you."

"That's okay. I got paid today." He hitched his chin to Blaine in thanks.

Her nephew. A paid employee on the ranch. Her heart swelled with pride for him.

"Well, keep your phone on and watch for my texts." She was sure there were a million things they should go over before he left. "And come find us if anything is… well, if you need me. We'll be walking around and sitting and…" An odd flutter in her chest kept her from forming a complete sentence. She wasn't used to having Connor go off with almost-strangers. The teens all seemed nice, but she didn't know them. Was she making a mistake?

"Thanks! I will." He tapped the pocket of his jeans, where he kept his phone. "I'll catch up with you later." Then he loped off toward the group.

Sienna didn't take her eyes off him until he caught up with the other teens.

She was worrying over nothing. Her sixteen-year-old nephew was plenty old enough to hang out with what seemed to be a nice group of teenagers without her getting all overprotective.

Still…she craned her neck to catch a glimpse of him. Their backs were to her as they headed toward the entrance.

"Well, should we try to find everyone?" Blaine, who

usually seemed so calm, had a nervous air about him tonight.

Reagan let out a resigned sigh. "I guess."

Surprised, Sienna studied her. She'd been under the impression Reagan was looking forward to the evening. She looked super cute in a lavender sundress with cowboy boots and a cowboy hat. Her long brown hair trailed down her back.

Sienna felt positively dowdy standing next to the slender beauty. She had worn a sundress, too, mainly because her maternity shorts tended to get tight around the thighs. But cute cowboy boots and cowboy hat? Nope. Her cushiony sandals and hair half pulled back would have to do.

She entwined her arm through Reagan's. "Your mom told me if I see a cute cowboy I have to give him your number."

"She did not." Her eyes widened in horror. Then she gave the ultimate eye roll.

Sienna laughed. "She did. I told her I'd keep an eye out for one."

"You do not want to date one of those players, Reagan." Blaine straightened—he had his intimidating big brother look on. Sienna would have chuckled if she didn't find it so endearing. She couldn't remember a time anyone had been overprotective of her.

"Like I would, Blaine." Reagan sounded exasperated. "I'm just here for the fries."

He narrowed his eyes at her, then, seemingly satisfied, looked around. "Ahh, there they are."

Mac and Bridget were holding hands and laughing at something. Sienna didn't see Sawyer and Tess yet. They were the only other couple attending. Randy and Hannah had a fishing trip planned up in Montana, and Jet and Holly had driven to Utah to see Holly's cousin.

"Where's Sawyer?" Blaine asked after everyone greeted each other with hugs.

Bridget sobered, looking at Mac, who addressed everyone. "Ken collapsed this afternoon. They don't know what's going on, so they're driving him to the hospital."

Reagan gasped, putting her hand over her mouth. Sienna remembered Tess telling Bridget her father wasn't doing very well. They hadn't spoken about it at the bonfire, but from what she'd pieced together he had lung cancer and had been in and out of treatment and remission for the past couple of years.

"Makes me wish the satellite cancer center was up and running now." Mac shook his head. "Sure would make it easier on them."

"What satellite cancer center?" Sienna asked. The group began moving in the direction of the entrance.

"I'm working with Hannah's brother—David Carr, a doctor in town—to build a small cancer clinic in Sunrise Bend. We've gotten two neighboring towns on board with sharing a team of traveling oncologists. David and I hired a management firm to oversee and manage the project."

"That's amazing." She could imagine the possibilities of having a rotating group of doctors. She was familiar with Dr. Carr, since she'd set up her prenatal appointments at his practice. "Are you building the clinic or renovating an existing space?"

"Renovating," Mac said. They joined the line of people waiting to get in. "We talked to the city council about having the clinic right downtown in one of my empty buildings. They voted on it and agreed."

"Well, if you need help finding grants for equipment and services, let me know. There are tons of them out there if you know where to look."

"Really?" He brightened. "That's good to know. I will. Thanks."

The line moved quickly, and soon Blaine had paid for both her and Reagan. Sienna tried to pay her own way, but he insisted.

Inside the fairgrounds, a line of food trucks were to the left, while covered bleachers were up ahead where the events would take place. Picnic tables and happy people were everywhere. The air smelled like cotton candy, horses and French fries. An odd combination... but not a bad one.

As Blaine strode purposefully to the truck marked French Fries, Sienna chuckled, glancing at Reagan. "He took your need for fries seriously, huh?"

Reagan smiled, making her even prettier than usual. "Believe it or not, Blaine hears everything, and he takes it to heart. That's why I love him."

She could see why Reagan loved him—it would be easy for Sienna to love him, too. A man who heard everything? Took it to heart? And actually acted on it?

Unheard of in her world.

They got in line with him. All around the park, lights blinked on overhead, adding to the festive atmosphere.

"What are you hungry for, Sienna?" Blaine asked as the line inched forward.

"I think your sister has the right idea. I'm getting an order of fries. And I would love one of those iced lemonades." She shouldn't be staring into his blue eyes, and she really shouldn't be noticing the spark in them when she mentioned the lemonade.

"Oh, I want an iced lemonade, too." Reagan nodded cheerfully.

"Why don't I get the lemonades while you two get the fries?" He angled his thumb in the direction of the lemonade stand.

"Sounds good." Reagan raised her hands near her chest and clapped twice, then turned to Sienna after Blaine was gone. "Maybe Mom's right. I should just find a cute cowboy and get it over with. I'm always torn. Sometimes I want a guy exactly like my brothers, which is idiotic. Jet's overbearing, and Blaine couldn't read between the lines if a cow was mooing in the middle of them. Then I look around Sunrise Bend and...ugh, I can't see a future with any of the men there. I'll never find a boyfriend or get married at this point."

Sienna had to make a concerted effort not to show her surprise. She'd never heard Reagan even mention guys or dating or marriage until now.

"Well, if you do find a guy like your brothers, snatch him up." She stepped forward as the line progressed. "I ended up with someone like neither of them, and I regret it."

She'd probably always regret it.

Troy had not been a good husband. He wouldn't make a good father. So why was she reluctant to help him waive his rights? Shouldn't she be dashing off a letter to her lawyer pronto? It would guarantee she'd never have to deal with her ex again. No texts, no calls, no custody, no child support.

She didn't know why she was hesitant, but she was.

"What was he like?" Reagan asked gently. "I'm sorry. Maybe you don't want to talk about him..."

"No, it's fine." She waved as if it was nothing. Maybe

it was. She didn't miss Troy. But she did miss her vision of the future with him.

Not that it would have been anything like what she'd imagined. She'd pictured him being home more, devoted to their child, a true husband and father.

A fantasy. Pure and simple. Her ex wasn't capable of any of that.

Maybe she should call her lawyer. Agree to his petition.

"Troy knows the right thing to say, but he never means it. Or maybe he means it for a minute. I don't know. I couldn't say. But he's up and down, hot and cold, thrilled to be with you one minute, running away the next. We had an entire relationship of weekends."

"A relationship of weekends? What does that mean?" Reagan turned to the window, where an older woman with a long, white ponytail asked for her order. "Three large fries, please."

"I've got this." Sienna dug out her wallet again and handed the lady some cash. "He drove trucks for a living. He was only home for a few weekends each month."

"Oh. I don't think I'd like that." She scrunched her nose, twisting her lips in sympathy.

"It's sad, Reagan, but after a while I preferred it." Admitting it out loud brought a spark of shame, but at least she was being honest.

"You don't miss him, then?"

"No. I miss who I thought he was."

"No chance of reconciliation?"

Sienna shuddered, shaking her head firmly. "No. It's over. Forever. I will never take him back."

"Here you go." Blaine suddenly reappeared, handing

Sienna a large lemonade. She flushed. How much of that had he heard?

"Thanks." She didn't meet his eyes. Did he think less of her for refusing to consider reconciling with Troy?

Maybe he hadn't overheard. But if he had? She wasn't giving elaborate explanations about her dysfunctional marriage at the rodeo.

"We got you a large fry, too." Reagan tore the paper off her straw.

"Great. I'm starving. Baling hay all week has been brutal."

"But you're finished now, right?" Sienna asked, thankful for the change of subject.

The ponytail lady handed them the fries, and they all turned to look for Mac and Bridget.

"Not quite," Blaine said. "We'll have everything done by early next week if it goes okay. I've already had to replace two parts. Thought I'd have to drag out Grandpa's ancient sickle mower for a minute there, but Jim and I got the swather back in action yesterday."

Sienna popped a hot fry in her mouth. *Salty, greasy— oh, my. So good.*

They spotted Mac and Bridget up ahead. Sienna gripped her lemonade in one hand and pressed the cup of fries in the crook of her arm in order to keep snacking as they walked.

"Holly said Jet was a positive bear yesterday." Reagan nibbled on a long, floppy French fry. "He thought he'd end up with more hay than he did. He was all mumbly and grouchy, and she told him to go ride around the ranch because she couldn't take his bad mood anymore."

"He didn't tell me any of that." Blaine frowned. "He acted like he'd baled the usual amount."

"Duh, of course, he did." His sister gave him an exasperated look. "You know how he is when it comes to the ranch."

He wore a confused expression. Reagan glanced up at him. "Jet never wants anyone worrying, and he takes it personal when anything goes wrong. So even if things aren't great, he pretends they are."

Sienna's stomach dropped at the description of Blaine's brother. She could see herself in those words, too. She didn't want Becca worrying about Connor or Lily. She didn't want Connor or Lily worrying about their parents. She certainly didn't want anyone worrying about her.

Even if things weren't great, Sienna pretended they were to protect everyone else.

"That's stupid." Blaine blew out a breath. "I flat-out told him I'm about a quarter shy of what I'd hoped to bale."

"That's because you're you," Reagan stated in a matter-of-fact tone.

His forehead furrowed, and Reagan must have thought that ended the conversation, because she moved on to ask Bridget what she got. Nachos, from the looks of it.

"I'm sorry you didn't end up with as much hay as you wanted." Sienna stared up at him. He was so solid. So handsome. So clearly bothered by the lack of hay…or by his brother. She couldn't tell. Maybe both.

"It's alright. I figured I wouldn't. I knew by the end of May when it hadn't rained, the harvest would be smaller than expected. I just didn't want to admit it."

"Nothing you can do about the weather." She nudged his arm with her elbow.

The corner of his mouth kicked up into a half-hearted smile. "I guess you're right."

The five of them meandered over to the stands and climbed the bleachers until they found a spot near the center about halfway up. Sienna set down her lemonade and tore into the fries with abandon. The events had already started, and she didn't bother to pay attention to the barrel racing in the arena. Her lower back had taken to aching in the evenings, and the bleachers weren't ideal, but at least she was sitting.

Blaine sat on one side of her, and Reagan on the other. Mac and Bridget were on Blaine's other side. As the events continued, Sienna and Reagan pointed out the horses they liked. She teased Blaine's sister about some of the cowboys, and Reagan would shake her head and grimace. All in all, it was a lot of fun.

Her phone vibrated and Becca's name appeared. On cue, her nerves went into overdrive. She never knew what she was going to get when Becca called.

"Hey, Bec."

"Where is Connor?" Becca's voice was shrill. "I've been trying to call him, and he's not answering. Did something happen?"

"He's fine." At least, she hoped he was. It wasn't like him to ignore his mother's calls. "We're at the rodeo. He probably didn't hear it ring."

"Oh, well put him on for me."

"I can't." Dread pooled in her stomach. She knew her sister well enough by now to know what was coming.

"Why not?"

"He's walking around with his new friends."

"Who are these friends? Why would you let him go off with strangers?"

"Calm down—"

"Don't tell me to calm down. I can't believe you. This is my son we're talking about."

She did not want to have an argument here. "I'll find him and have him call you."

"If he's not on the phone with me in five minutes, I'll drive up there myself."

Her jaw ached she was clenching it so tightly. "There's no need—"

"I can't even with you right now. Five minutes." And the line went dead.

Blaine was watching her. "Is everything okay?"

A million thoughts crowded through her mind. *Had* she been reckless? Was Becca right that she shouldn't have let him go off with a bunch of kids she didn't know? Hadn't she thought the same thing herself?

She hefted herself up, wincing as she placed her hand on her lower back. "I need to find Connor. Becca's worried."

"I'll help." He immediately stood, taking her elbow to steady her.

"Want me to come, too?" Reagan asked.

"No, you stay," Sienna said. "This shouldn't take long."

She and Blaine made their way down the bleachers and out of the stands. "I'm going to text him."

"I can have Mac text Kaylee, too. I should have thought of that a few minutes ago."

"It's okay." She texted Connor. Where are you? Your mom is worried.

What if something had happened with him and the group? Had he gotten separated from them? Was he in trouble?

In her heart, she knew he was enjoying himself. Couldn't he be a regular teenager for once? He probably didn't answer Becca's call because he didn't want his mom to spoil the evening.

A text came back immediately from him. Sorry. We were looking at the horses in the stables.

Relief flooded her swiftly, a welcome sensation from the earlier dread. It's okay. Can you call her? Like right now?

She stretched her neck from side to side as she waited for a reply. Yeah.

"He's calling her." She spun to Blaine, not realizing how close he was. He reached out, taking hold of her raised forearms before she landed in his chest. "Oof… I'm sorry."

"Don't be." His voice was husky, his skin warm. Those strong hands loosened their grip, caressing her arms as they slid away. His touch surprised her in the best possible way. But it threw her off balance, too.

It would be so easy to rely on Blaine. But it wouldn't be fair to either of them.

She backed up quickly, directing her attention to her phone. "Let me ask him to text me after he calls her."

His eyes glimmered with appreciation, and she had to look away again.

No, no, no. Blaine Mayer was off-limits.

He tempted her to want things she couldn't have.

A husband, a father for her baby, a steady man who would actually treat her like she was important to him.

She had a life in Casper to return to in a month. She couldn't afford fantasies at this point in her life. They'd only hurt her. And she'd been hurt enough.

Blaine could barely concentrate in church on Sunday morning. He'd opted for the early service while everyone else in his family, along with Sienna and the kids, had committed to the late service. He was glad to be alone. He needed some space to process a few things.

What Reagan had said so nonchalantly at the rodeo Friday night had been gnawing at him, but all day yesterday he'd been busy trying to finish up the hay, so he'd pushed it from his mind.

When she'd told him about Jet being upset about his own hay output, why had he been so surprised? Logically, Blaine knew his brother was up against the same weather conditions as the rest of the county. Yet, when Jet didn't say anything about baling less than usual, Blaine had assumed he'd baled more than him. And Reagan had practically rolled her eyes when she'd said, "That's because you're you." What had she meant by that?

He'd never been good at reading between the lines. He just assumed when the people closest to him said something, they were telling him the truth. If they left something out, he wasn't aware of it. Not that everyone was transparent. He wasn't stupid.

Maybe Jet hadn't intended to mislead him. Reagan's assessment about their brother not wanting anyone to worry rang true. Jet always put up a brave front. Even when things weren't as fine as he made them seem.

But surely, he understood he didn't have to hide anything from Blaine.

He didn't need to be protected. He was a grown man. And besides, they were more than brothers. They were best friends.

The congregation rose to pray. He joined them, trying to follow along and failing spectacularly. His mind was jumbled. All his life he'd been two steps behind his big brother. And all his life he'd tried to keep up but couldn't.

He turned his attention to the service folder for the responsive reading. When it was over, everyone sat, and the pastor began the sermon.

"We sure could use some rain," the pastor said. "I've been hearing those words for a few months now. If we had a show of hands, I'm sure every one of yours would be in the air if you've heard or said them, too."

A chuckle rippled through the pews.

"We sure could use some rain." His voice softened as he shook his head. "Drought in Wyoming is nothing new. And there is still time for it to turn around. A couple of rainfalls could make a world of difference for our neighbors. It would green up the grazing land, water our gardens, replenish the reservoirs."

Blaine found himself nodding. The pastor was speaking his language.

"But what if we don't get a couple of rainfalls? What if we don't get any rain?"

His stomach twisted. He might have to consider selling off some of the herd, and he wasn't prepared to make those decisions.

"Is God any less faithful? When we go through rough patches or complete devastation, does it mean God no longer loves us?"

Blaine couldn't help thinking of Cody. The day his brother drove away in fury. The texts and calls Cody had ignored. The day they'd found out he'd been killed in a head-on collision. The afternoon Jet had brought Holly and Clara to the ranch, when none of them had known Cody had even been married, let alone had a child. And the hardest one of all—when they'd learned his brother had pretended they didn't exist.

"...spiritual drought is worse than a physical one.

Isaiah, chapter forty-three, verses eighteen and nine-
teen states 'Remember ye not the former things, neither consider the things of old. Behold, I will do a new
thing—now it shall spring forth, shall ye not know it?
I will even make a way in the wilderness, and rivers in
the desert.' Now before you get excited about rivers in
the desert, the context of these verses is important. The
Israelites had turned away from God…"

Blaine balled his hands into fists, squeezing until his
fingernails dug into his palms.

He hadn't turned away from God. But his brother
was dead.

He'd prayed for rain. But the harvest was sparse.

He'd been trying to fight his feelings for Sienna. But
they were still there.

As the pastor continued to speak, Blaine's mind wandered to the tail end of Sienna's conversation with Reagan at the rodeo that he'd have to have been deaf not to
hear. She'd been adamant she would never take back her
ex-husband. That it was over. Forever.

His heart squeezed, wringing out like a dishrag.

Forever was a long time to cut someone you once
loved out of your life.

He should know. His brother had cut him out in a split
second and never looked back.

Everyone was rising once more. Blaine lurched to his
feet. So much for listening to the sermon.

*Lord, I'm sorry. I came here to worship, and all I
did was fret and think about things I don't need to be
thinking about.*

The rest of the service passed quickly, and he quietly
sang along to the final worship song before everyone
was dismissed. Blaine kept the small talk with people

light as he made his way to the front entrance and out the door. He descended the concrete porch steps, catching up to Austin, who had AJ on his hip and a baby blue diaper bag over his shoulder.

"Hey, man, how's it going?" Blaine fell into step next to him. "And how's our little buddy doing?"

"Good." The lines in Austin's face said otherwise. "We're good, aren't we, AJ?"

The boy had celebrated his first birthday a few months ago. Now he buried his face in Austin's shoulder.

"Actually, Blaine, I'm not good." They continued slowly walking toward the parking lot. "Did you get your hay in?"

"Yeah." He ground his teeth together. It was still a sore subject. Probably would be until next spring.

"Me, too. I... Well, I came up pretty short." Austin pressed the button to unlock his truck. A beeping sound came from halfway up one of the rows of parking spaces. The sun was already hot, and the lack of a breeze was stifling.

"Tell me about it." Blaine was glad he wasn't the only one, but he didn't want to wish it on his friends, either.

"What the pastor said back there got me to thinking."

Which part? Again, Blaine felt foolish for not listening better.

"About God doing a new thing. What if this new thing is bad?"

They reached Austin's truck, and he opened the back door, setting AJ into his car seat. The boy protested, and Austin made quick work of buckling him in, kissing his forehead and shutting the door, then turning back to Blaine.

"I don't think that's what you were supposed to get out of it." But what did he know?

"Yeah, you're right." He shook his head, looking flushed. "Forget it."

"No, wait. What were you thinking?"

"Just that life's been changing nonstop for a year, and frankly, I can deal with most of it. But this drought…"

"Yeah, I know." Blaine felt it, too. "I don't know about you, but I'm going to pray for rain."

"I was thinking the same." Austin gave him a slight smile. "Do you think God will listen?"

"He always listens. He just doesn't always answer the way we want."

"That's what I'm afraid of."

"We'll get through it." Blaine rested his hand on Austin's shoulder. "We always do."

"You're right." They stood there for a moment until Austin broke the silence. "You still have any of those puppies left?"

"I do." Blaine hadn't put any effort into trying to find homes for them. He'd better start spreading the word about the pups soon, or he'd be stuck with six Aussies come August. "I have six to choose from."

"I'm tempted to have you pick me out a male."

"Tricolor or blue merle?"

"If AJ was older, I'd want a blue merle." He shrugged. "I could use another good herding dog, but I think taking care of a puppy and AJ would be beyond me at this point."

"I might continue to breed Tiara. Haven't made up my mind."

"You'll have no trouble finding homes for them if

you do." Austin opened the driver's side door. "Are you going to the Fourth of July festival?"

"Of course." He'd have to talk to Sienna about bringing Connor and Lily. The festival was just over a week away. The puppies would be old enough to leave for a few hours if his dad didn't want to watch them.

"Good. I'll see you then."

Blaine waved goodbye and made his way to his truck. The summer was passing quickly. Only a little more than a month before Sienna and the kids would return to Casper.

He frowned, not liking the thought. He'd been enjoying having them around. Connor had effortlessly gotten into the rhythm of ranch life, and Lily had been indispensable with the puppies.

And then there was Sienna.

Independent, but not afraid to ask for his help. Generous, but not a pushover.

And alone during what should be a special time in her life. She deserved a partner. But he didn't think she wanted one. And he didn't want to be the next guy she cut out of her life forever.

So he might as well make peace with the fact she'd be gone soon. It wasn't like he had any choice in the matter.

Chapter Eight

If her stomach got any bigger, she'd be a danger to society.

Independence Day had arrived hot and sunny. Sienna waited for Blaine to come around to the passenger side of his truck to help her down. Connor and Lily were already standing near the truck bed in the large parking lot behind the feed store in downtown Sunrise Bend. Blaine offered her his hand, and a rush of appreciation filled her as he gently helped her step to the ground.

The sounds of a band warming up and distant laughter from the carnival, along with the delicious smells of barbecue and funnel cakes, filled the air. She had a feeling she'd be eating her way around the Fourth of July festival with Blaine. She glanced at him. Steady as ever. What she wouldn't give for some of that steadiness herself.

The longer she stayed in Sunrise Bend, the more she dreaded returning to Casper with its responsibilities and problems. But mostly she dreaded it because he wouldn't be there.

"I see Lydia and Kaylee," Connor said, pointing. "Come on, Lil, let's go."

"Make sure you check your phones, guys!" Sienna called. They were already jogging away. "And pick up if your mom calls."

Connor looked over his shoulder, gave her a thumbs-up and yelled, "We will!"

"Can't get away from us fast enough, can they?" Blaine gaped as Connor and Lily weaved through families to get to their friends.

"No, they can't." Sienna had worn a long sundress with sandals. Beads of sweat were already forming at the base of her neck. "It's going to be a hot one."

They slowly walked across the parking lot. Their destination was Main Street, where the food trucks and vendors had set up in the middle of the blocked-off road.

"Connor seems better today," Blaine said.

"Yeah, I'm glad." Becca had called Connor two days ago and unloaded about how Aaron criticized her in couples' therapy. Sienna had heard the entire call because she'd been sitting on the porch's rocking chair near the open window, where Connor had been sitting on the couch next to Ollie.

He'd been quiet and gloomy all day yesterday.

She wasn't sure how to handle the situation. This was his mother—her sister—whom they both loved very much. Sienna had told him on more than one occasion that he didn't have to listen to every complaint. He could set limits and still love his mom. But had she gotten through to him?

"Lily doesn't get her calls?" Blaine took her by the elbow, protecting her from a group of fast-moving adolescents, as they headed down the side street.

"Becca calls Lily, but they talk about normal stuff, like the puppies," she said. "Thank you, by the way, for assuring her you're going to find the puppies homes. I think it will be easier for her to leave them if she knows they each have a new family lined up."

"Yeah, well, I thought she was going to start crying when I mentioned selling Sushi. That little guy means the world to her."

"I know. It's going to be hard when we leave." In more ways than one. Sienna pointed up ahead. "Come on, let's go find your mom and sister's table." Mayer Canyon Candles had sponsored a booth, and Reagan had made special red-white-and-blue striped candles for the occasion.

They made it to Main Street and strolled past a variety of vendors selling handmade leather goods, collectibles, homemade jams and other items. Soon, they spotted Reagan. They waited until the line of customers dwindled before chatting with her for a while and asking if she needed anything. She declined, pointing to a box of donuts Hannah had dropped off earlier. After several minutes, Sienna sensed Blaine getting antsy next to her. They waved goodbye and turned in the direction of the food.

"I'm starving," Blaine said. "Let's grab a bite to eat."

"You read my mind."

"Why don't we go to the community center? They serve up a full meal, and we can sit under their tent, get out of the heat."

"That sounds amazing." She was glad he wasn't rushing. His long legs would have outpaced her even when she wasn't pregnant, and every week she got bigger and slower.

Up ahead, she spotted Lily laughing with Kaylee near

the shaved-ice truck. Connor and Bryce, whom she recognized from the ranch, were joking around next to them with Lydia and a few other boys and girls. Sienna smiled and waved at Lily, who waved back.

The sight of them enjoying themselves satisfied her in a way she couldn't describe. This was why she'd come here. She nudged Blaine and pointed to the group of teens. "You were right. This will be a summer to remember."

He turned his attention to where she pointed. "It's not hard when school's out, they can spend time with friends and the weather's good."

"True." They continued their slow stroll to the community center. "Thank you for bringing me here. I'm sure you have better things to do."

"I don't. I'd rather be with you."

Her cheeks grew warm. "That's the nicest thing anyone's said to me in a long time."

"I hope you don't mean that."

Sadly, she did. Between her sister's tunnel vision about Aaron and her own preoccupation about Connor and Lily, Sienna had grown used to feeling like the happiness of her loved ones rested on her shoulders. So to think someone wanted to be around her when she was plagued with worries was pleasant to hear, and she found herself wanting to open up to Blaine, to share more about her life.

"My ex-husband, Troy—" she kept her chin high "—wasn't around much. I got used to seeing him only a weekend here or a weekend there, and I'm afraid I grew independent."

"You say that like it's a bad thing."

They reached the community center's lawn, where a

large white tent had been set up. A line formed at a table in front of the entrance. They reached the end and stood behind a middle-aged couple.

"I don't know. If I had needed Troy more or if he had been around more..." She swallowed, unsure why it bothered her to talk about it. "If I had been less independent, maybe things would have been different..."

"Why wasn't he around?"

"His job. He drove long-distance for a trucking company."

"Then he didn't stay away because of you." Blaine stared ahead. "He didn't know how blessed he was. If he did, he would have been around more, wouldn't have let you go."

Her heartbeat fluttered as her breath caught. Did Blaine have any idea how much her parched heart was soaking up his words?

"I don't know if he was capable. He had issues." She didn't want to pull a Becca and bad-mouth her ex, but she also wanted Blaine to know the truth. "One minute he would be so icy cold I'm surprised I didn't get frostbite. An hour later, he was bouncing with excitement, wanting to spend time with me. It was confusing."

"Why would he do that?"

They were next in line. She shuffled forward. "After our wedding, I suspected he had a personality disorder of some sort. He got so angry when I brought it up, though, I didn't make that mistake again. Anyway, he recently confirmed it."

"Is that why you broke up?"

"No." She glanced up at him. She couldn't tell him here. Not this close to the other people waiting to pay.

Blaine took out his wallet, and Sienna handed him a

twenty. He shook his head as if he'd never seen or heard of such a thing as her paying for her own meal. Then he placed his hand at the small of her back to urge her forward.

His simple touch loosened the grip she had on keeping her failed marriage in the past, where it belonged. She'd tell him the rest before she lost her nerve. The beverage station was deserted at the moment, so she wandered to the table where ice-cold pitchers of water, lemonade and iced tea were placed. Blaine stayed by her side. When she was sure they were alone, she faced him.

"Troy left me the day I told him I was pregnant." She watched his face for his reaction. Disbelief mingled with anger. "He told me it was over. He was filing for divorce and he wanted nothing—and I mean nothing—to do with our unborn child."

"What?" he hissed. "Why?"

She shrugged, reaching for the metal pitcher of lemonade. Beads of water dotted the side of it. "I hoped he was going through one of his hot-and-cold phases. What I didn't know was he had a girlfriend. A much older girlfriend. I'm not proud to admit that fact didn't shock me as much as him telling me he wanted to legally waive his parental rights."

Blaine tensed as he drew himself to his full height. "Did he?" His voice was razor-sharp and low. "Waive them?"

"He's trying to." As each day passed, she became more confused about what to do. What would be best for the baby? What would be best for her? And…what would be best for Troy? She didn't know at this point. "I feel bad saying this, but in some ways having him out of the picture for good would make my life easier."

Glass of lemonade in hand, she turned, her belly bumping a pitcher of water in the process. Blaine reached out and steadied it.

"Let's eat before I knock over the entire table." She injected levity in her tone. Opening up about the less savory parts of her past was difficult. "I didn't mean to dump all this on you."

He didn't respond, just plucked the lemonade from her hand and set it on a nearby table, where there were several seats open. "You sit. I'll get us food."

For once, she didn't argue. She let him take the lead and hoped he wasn't put off by what she'd told him.

As Blaine loaded two paper plates with shredded pork sandwiches, mac and cheese, coleslaw and cornbread, he tried to wrap his head around what Sienna had just told him.

Her ex had cheated on her? With an older woman? And didn't want to claim his own child?

He nodded his thanks to the workers refilling the warming trays of food and returned to the table with plastic silverware packets tucked into his pocket and both hands holding their plates. He set down one plate in front of Sienna, put the other at his spot across from her and slid one of the silverware packets her way before taking a seat.

"Oh, wow, this looks yummy." She took a bite of the mac and cheese.

He let his food sit there a moment as he watched her intently. No one else was sharing their table, but he kept his voice low just in case.

"Explain this waiving-parental-rights thing." He had

to know more. Normally, he'd let the subject drop, but it felt too important.

She finished her bite, patted the napkin to her lips and set it back down. "It means what it sounds like. He would have no rights or obligations regarding the baby."

"No custody?"

"Correct."

"What about child support?"

She shook her head.

He slumped back in his seat, stunned. "I didn't know that was a thing."

"I didn't, either." Her voice was so soft, he almost couldn't hear her. "It's irrevocable. If the court agrees to it, he can't change his mind."

"Good."

"For me, maybe. But what about the baby?" The look she gave him was heavy. "I never wanted my child to not have a father, you know?"

"Some father. On the road all the time and dating a nursing-home patient." The words were out before he thought them through. He winced, unable to bring himself to see her reaction. He wasn't trying to hurt her.

At the odd, strangled sound coming from her throat, he glanced up. She had her hand over her mouth and appeared to be...laughing? No, that couldn't be.

But her face grew red as she tried to stifle the laugh, then she took away her hand and shook her head. Yep, she was laughing. He couldn't prevent his own grin from spreading. He tore off a chunk of cornbread and popped it into his mouth.

"Thanks, Blaine." She sighed, tucking the fork into the coleslaw. "I know you're right. And to be honest, any relationship Troy would have with our child would be unpredictable. I don't really want that for my baby, either—a lifetime of broken promises. I'm under no illusions about my ex. He'll lavish you with attention one minute and miss your birthday two days later. It was hard enough dealing with it as his wife. I can't imagine a child trying to navigate it."

Blaine kept his mouth shut, or he'd release the string of unkind words sitting on the tip of his tongue. Sienna had enough to deal with. He took a big bite of his pork sandwich.

"I keep wanting the baby to have some semblance of a normal life—what other kids have, you know?" Her elbow was resting on the table, white plastic fork dangling from her fingers. "But it puts me in a tough spot. My lawyer needs to know if I'll support Troy's petition. He finally went to the doctor and was officially diagnosed with a personality disorder, so the courts might allow him to waive his rights. But if I support his petition, it will increase his chances of them ruling in his favor."

He tried to put himself in her shoes, but he couldn't. It seemed like her life would be less of a hassle without her ex-husband in it. But what did he know?

"It would be tough explaining his absence," she said. "I mean, how do you tell your own kid their father cut himself out of their life on purpose? I've been down a similar road, and it hurts. It hurts so much."

Blaine stopped chewing, the bite of food tasting like cardboard all of a sudden. He knew what it was like to be cut out of someone's life on purpose, too. And he still hadn't recovered.

"Who cut you out of their life?" He resumed chewing and watched her. He didn't know much about her past, other than she'd come to live with her grandmother back in high school, and after the grandma died, Sienna had moved to Casper.

"I'm sure we've talked enough about me." She averted her gaze. "What about you? Obviously, you're single. I hope you had better taste in women than I did in Troy."

She wanted to know about his dating life? He lunged for his glass of water, taking a gulp, since not a single thought on how to reply came into his head.

"It's been a while since I've dated anyone." The truth was the easiest to say. "Mom and Holly want that to change. They're always talking about how I should call this girl or that one. None of them are my type." He shouldn't have admitted all that.

"What is your type?" Her big green eyes were clear, open, inviting. It would be the simplest thing in the world to reach across the table and take her hand in his. *You. You're my type.*

"Not who they're talking about," he said gruffly. "I've got a ranch to run, anyhow."

"You can't run a ranch and have a girlfriend?"

No, he couldn't. "I don't think so."

"Look at Sawyer and Tess. And Jet and Holly. And Mac and Bridget." She took another bite of her sandwich.

Thinking of his friends getting picked off one by one by the ladies made him grimace. They'd all found real love. Lasting love.

He didn't know if it was possible for him.

And the only one who tempted him to find out was sitting across from him, seven months pregnant with no plans to stay.

The fireworks were set to begin in fifteen minutes. Sienna was lounging in a camping chair with Tess on one side and Reagan on the other. Holly and Bridget were on the other side of Tess, and Hannah chatted with Cassie—Austin's nanny for AJ—on a quilt spread out in front of the chairs. The half moon was already shining brightly above them as the constellations blinked on, one star at a time. Today had been amazing. And challenging, exciting, nerve-wracking and eye-opening.

Something had shifted within her. Something she didn't want to dwell on.

It was too scary to contemplate.

She looked around for Connor. He was watching the fireworks with his friends nearby. Even from here, she could tell he was enjoying himself as he joked around with them. Lily had returned to the ranch with Julie and Kevin earlier. Her niece had had a fun time, too, but in her words, she needed to get back to the puppies.

"So, Reagan, I noticed how Brad Sanders was eyeing you earlier." Tess bent forward to talk to Reagan with Sienna between them. "I hope he asked you out."

Reagan stiffened. "He did not. And I don't want him to."

Tess laughed mischievously. "I think you'd have a good time. And don't even try to say he isn't cute."

Reagan leaned closer to Sienna, keeping her voice low. "He dated all of my friends in high school. Every one of them. I would never go out with him."

Sienna stifled a laugh.

Holly, perking up at the talk of Reagan dating, scooted her chair closer to Tess's to hear better. "What about Tim Evans?"

Reagan glared at her. "Holly, I love you like a sister. I'm glad Jet married you. But if I ever hear you mention

Tim Evans to me as a potential date again, I'm disowning you."

Holly rolled her eyes, shaking her head. Again, Sienna laughed. Who knew Reagan could be this assertive when it came to dating?

"What's wrong with Tim?" Holly asked, unfazed by her speech.

"What's right with him?"

"He owns a successful business."

"He's a mortician. I don't see myself living in a funeral home."

Holly's face fell. "But—"

"No." Reagan leaned in to Sienna again. "I'm this close to inventing a boyfriend, just to get everyone off my back."

"Blaine said something similar earlier." Sienna's gaze zoomed to where he and his buddies were standing, not too far from the ladies, talking, laughing and waiting for the fireworks.

"Yeah, well, no one's harassing him now that you're here." She reached down for her bottle of water, and Sienna was thankful for the darkness. Did they think she and Blaine could be a couple? For real?

Her heart flipped at the thought. It had been what she'd been fighting for days—this feeling, this longing for the real thing.

Blaine was the real thing.

Maybe it was the fact he was a cowboy, devoted to the land and the animals on it. Or maybe it was their history—the easy companionship and fun they'd had in high school. His handsome face, strong arms and beautiful blue eyes were all factors, too. But she wasn't one to be swayed by looks.

No, it was his personality, his way of taking life as it came, his solidness—those were the things that captured her heart and wouldn't let her go.

She was falling for Blaine Mayer.

And she couldn't stop it.

In a few short weeks, she and the kids would pack up and leave. She'd have her baby. Resume her job at the college. Be available for Connor, Lily and Becca, whenever they needed her.

She'd lost her father, her mother, her grandmother. She wouldn't lose the rest of her family, too.

Why was she thinking about it now, anyhow? She was surrounded by new friends, enjoying a gorgeous summer night. This wasn't the place to be reflecting on life.

She needed a distraction. Badly.

"What does your ideal boyfriend look like?" Sienna asked Reagan.

"I don't care what he looks like. He'd just better be able to handle me."

Handle her? Gentle, creative, sweet Reagan? What guy wouldn't be able to? She was like a dream come true.

"In what way?" Sienna asked.

"I don't put up with cheating."

"I don't, either."

"I have to work nights and weekends sometimes when we're busy, so he has to understand the business is important to me."

"Sounds reasonable. I think most guys would understand."

"I'd want my parents to like him. And he, them."

"Your parents are easy to love." Sienna tried to suppress the regret that she'd never known Troy's parents.

He wouldn't speak of his mom and had no contact with his father.

"A guy who's honest, too."

"That goes without saying," Sienna said. "And I think he should be cute. You deserve a gorgeous guy."

Reagan chuckled and squeezed her arm. "Thanks, Sienna. I needed that."

A popping sound had them all gazing up at the sky. The first fireworks display exploded in white streamers. It was followed by starbursts of green and ribbons of red and blue.

"Are you doing okay?" Blaine said near her ear.

She startled, turning her head, surprised to see him crouching behind her, his eyes watching her intently.

"I'm great. Aren't the fireworks pretty?"

He didn't respond, but she could feel his warm breath near her cheek. It tempted her to lean back and let her cheek touch his. And that thought had her picturing pressing her lips to his.

Stop it!

She fanned herself, then realized she looked idiotic and clasped her hands around the arms of the chair.

"Are you too hot? I can take you home if you'd like." There was that breath on her cheek again. Didn't the man understand how attracted she was to him? How much she was starting to need him?

"I'm not hot. I want to stay."

"I'm right here if you need me." He shifted to one knee, staying close to her chair. Impulsively, she grabbed his hand and squeezed it. He gave her a surprised glance.

But he didn't take his hand away.

Instead, he entwined his fingers with hers. Her gaze

remained trained on the sky, but she didn't register any more fireworks.

Because Blaine Mayer was holding her hand. And it was the most romantic thing she'd ever experienced.

Tomorrow, she'd talk herself out of these feelings. But tonight, she'd hold his hand under a sky popping with fireworks. And she'd tuck away the memory to cherish for years to come.

Chapter Nine

"Alright, Connor, let's go over the game plan." On Friday Blaine, Jim and Connor stood outside one of the corrals. The bulls had an air of excitement about them. Blaine was convinced they always knew when they were about to be pastured with the cows. "Today is kind of like the beginning of the year for the ranch."

"What do you mean?" Connor turned off the UTV and stood next to it, waiting for further instruction.

"The cycle starts all over again," Jim said. He'd driven the four-wheeler over. "The bulls join the cows, and soon we'll have a herd of pregnant cows again."

"We need to be cautious," Blaine said. "When feeling threatened, cows run. But bulls? They want to fight. So we're going to rely on the older bulls to help the younger ones see the trailer as nonthreatening." He checked the hitch where the trailer was attached to the truck. Everything appeared to be ready. "I'll back the trailer to the gate, and Jim will take the four-wheeler to steer them through the series of corrals. Your job is to open and close the gates. As soon as you open one, climb up on the fence. I don't want you getting hurt. I'll be behind the bulls with a long paddle to keep them moving. Let's hope none of them get cold feet about getting in the trailer."

"Will they all fit?" Connor asked. Jim gunned the four-wheeler and drove along the fence to the gate of the large corral, where the bulls were milling about.

"No. We'll be taking more than one load. I'm glad the weather is perfect. I would have waited until next week if it was too hot or windy, or even too cold. They get ornery easily."

"What else should I do?"

"Keep an eye out for us. If one of the bulls is getting close, holler."

"Okay."

"Go ahead and drive over there." He pointed to the smallest corral. "Once I back the trailer to the gate, I'll need your help getting it lined up."

He nodded and started the UTV. Blaine climbed into the truck for the short drive. Ever since the fireworks, he'd been busy moving the bales of hay to winter storage. He'd still had too much time to think about Sienna, though, and everything he'd learned about her.

What she'd told him about her ex-husband had curdled his stomach. She deserved better than that.

And what she'd said about wanting her baby to have a father? He hadn't been able to stop thinking about it. He tried not to let his mind wander to kids or having a family. Mainly because he'd never really wanted to get married.

But Sienna had him questioning himself.

If the impossible happened and somehow they ended up together...could he be a father to someone else's child? Could he be a father period?

Checking his mirrors, he backed up the trailer, then rolled down his window.

"How much room do I have?" he yelled to Connor, who was standing near the gate. Connor used his hands to show him the distance. Blaine nodded. "Do I need to go to the right or left?"

He pointed to the left. Soon, the trailer was flush against the wooden gate. Blaine cut the engine and got out of the truck, striding over to Connor.

"You can slide it open." While Connor took care of the gate, Blaine got on his two-way radio and told Jim they were almost ready. Then he and Connor drove the UTV back to the big corral.

Blaine understood Sienna's devotion to Connor and Lily. They were good kids, and Blaine wanted the best for them, too. He and Connor had discussed his home life on several occasions as they'd ridden out to check cattle. It sounded like his mom wanted to stay married to his dad, but Connor was worried his dad didn't feel the same. Blaine had nodded and muttered something about relationships being complicated, but what else could he say? He didn't have much experience in the matter.

He felt awkward in those situations. Like with Sienna. She'd shared deeply personal things about her marriage and ex-husband, and he hadn't reassured her. He'd just blurted out exactly what was on his mind. Although, he had to admit, Sienna had been amused. And she was the one who'd reached for his hand at the fireworks. Hadn't pulled away, either.

Was he reading too much into it?

The first bulls were approaching the gate as Connor straddled the fence nearby. On the four-wheeler, Jim blocked most of the bulls from retreating, but one escaped, and being the expert he was, Jim wheeled back around and herded it with the rest of them.

"Okay, Connor, go ahead and shut it!" Blaine yelled when they were all through. "Then hustle to the next gate and do the same thing."

They continued moving the bulls until the trailer was full. Then Blaine drove Connor and Jim several miles away to where the cows were pastured, stopping the truck at a distance from the herd.

"Why did you park so far away?" Connor asked, getting out of the truck. They all went to the back of the trailer.

"It's better to let them come together naturally." Jim shifted his cowboy hat back as he squinted to the herd. "Don't want any of 'em fighting."

"Stay back." Blaine waved for Connor to keep his distance while he opened the trailer door. The bulls meandered out and seemed to know exactly where to go, grazing as they went. The three of them watched for a while, and Blaine sighed in relief as the bulls mingled with the cows. So far, the day had gone according to plan.

"Looks like there won't be trouble." Jim reached for the passenger door. "Let's get the rest of 'em taken care of."

"Blaine?" Connor asked from the back seat as they drove back.

"Yeah?"

"Have you decided if you're keeping Tiara and Ollie? You know, to continue breeding them?"

He cringed. He'd been avoiding thinking about the subject. Tiara was healthy. And Ollie had proven his worth as a herding dog time and again since arriving.

But without Lily around to help with the puppies, could Blaine continue breeding them? Sure, his dad helped a lot, but Lily did many of the tasks Blaine would have to do with future litters. Like weighing them, watching over them, making sure they all met their milestones. She even groomed Tiara every day.

Lily was passionate about puppy care. And Blaine was passionate about the ranch.

"I don't know yet, Connor."

"Oh." He sounded disappointed. "What will happen to them if you don't keep them?"

"Laura would find another breeder. She won't separate them."

"Ollie's happy here."

Blaine looked at him in the rearview. His chin was tucked. It was obvious the kid had bonded with Ollie. Lily had told him the dog slept at the foot of Connor's bed each night.

It was going to be hard on all of them—the dogs included—when Sienna and the teens left. At least they still had some things to look forward to before they returned to Casper. Tomorrow the four of them were riding out to one of his favorite spots on the ranch and having a picnic. The kids wanted to take out the four-wheelers, and he'd told Sienna he'd take her in his truck, since it would be more comfortable.

"I promise you I will not make the decision lightly," Blaine said, meeting his eyes in the mirror. "The dogs are important. I want what's best for them. And if I can't give them what's best for them, I'll make sure they go to someone who can."

He wasn't sure he could give anyone what was best for them.

Wouldn't Sienna be better off near her family? Wouldn't her child be better off having a father in its life? Wouldn't the dogs be better off with someone passionate about breeding them? Someone who could give them the care and devotion Lily did?

He was stretched thin as it was. It wouldn't be smart to stretch himself even thinner. The people and animals depending on him deserved better than that.

Sienna drank in the view as Blaine kept his truck at a distance behind Connor and Lily, both on four-wheelers, on their way to the picnic spot the next day. Wyoming was truly wide-open country. To the left, mountains created a jagged edge where they met the sky. To the right, pastures revealed cattle either grazing or lying down. They looked like lumps of black-and-brown from her position. A slender blue ribbon of a creek that hadn't completely dried up came into view.

The truck handled the terrain with ease. Both windows were open, allowing a breeze to flow through the cab.

She and Blaine hadn't spoken much since the festival. And they'd only said a few words today. The silence wasn't awkward, though. It never was with him. It had been a full week since the fireworks, and she was glad to be out of her normal routine. A picnic miles away from civilization under a big blue sky was exactly what she needed.

"Connor said you got all the bulls out to pasture with the cows yesterday." Sienna had enjoyed hearing her nephew explain the process last night while Lily attempted to sketch Sushi from memory.

"We did. He was a big help." Blaine glanced over at

her with a grin. "Did he tell you about the young bull we introduced to the heifers?"

"No." She shifted to watch him. The corners of his eyes crinkled. He seemed younger, happier when he talked about the bulls. "What happened?"

"Well, Jim and I thought the bull wasn't quite ready for the herd, so we figured the heifers would help get him used to the idea. Let's just say the ladies were really interested in him, and the poor fellow wasn't sure what to make of it. He turned around to flee, and they ganged up on him, sniffing him all the way. It was pretty funny."

She chuckled. "I'm sure. Do you think he'll get used to them?"

"He already has. I checked on him this morning. He looked content."

"Well, good." Her phone vibrated. Becca's name appeared. She ignored it. They'd spoken for an hour last night, mostly about Aaron possibly moving back in. Sienna hoped he would. She wanted them to be a family again. "Have you been able to find the puppies homes? Lily's worried about what will happen to them."

He winced. "Not yet. I've been in contact with the two people Ralph promised. Now that the bulls are taken care of and the hay is in, I can focus more on finding the puppies homes. You do know Lily's never going to be okay with Sushi being sold, right?"

"I know."

They kept following the kids, and Sienna checked her phone once more. Becca had texted her. Troy stopped by earlier. Thought you'd want to know. Call me when you get a minute.

The bottom dropped out of her stomach. She didn't

want Troy bothering her sister or giving Becca some sob story about how heartless she was.

"What's wrong? You look like you're in pain." Blaine frowned.

"No, nothing like that. It's my ex. He stopped over at my sister's place."

"I thought he was out of the picture."

"Like I said before, he's hot and cold, either clinging or distant." The thought hit her that maybe he'd gone to Becca's to convince her to pressure Sienna into supporting him waiving his parental rights. "I hate to do this, but would you mind if I call her back really quick?"

"Go ahead."

She pressed Becca's number. It rang until it went to voice mail. "Hey, it's me. Call me back when you get this. I'm sorry Troy bothered you."

"Has she been okay lately?" Blaine asked. "Connor's been in a good mood."

"Yeah, she has." Sienna placed her hand on her belly. "I talked to her yesterday. She thinks Aaron will be moving back in soon."

"That's good news."

"Yes, it is. If it really happens."

"Why wouldn't it?"

How could she explain? Her childhood had been splintered. Becca's had, too. And the wounds from it affected everything. It was hard for them to trust other people's words. Maybe if he had some background, he'd understand.

"You know my brother drowned when I was four, right?"

His shocked face told her he hadn't known. Why

would he, though? She hadn't felt comfortable talking about it until she was an adult.

"It devastated our family. Becca was closer to him than I was. She's eight years older than me and was three years older than Dan. I feel like everyone blamed each other and also themselves when it happened. Dan was a decent swimmer, so no one noticed when he swam farther out than he should have. We were at a reservoir. They think he got a cramp and couldn't make his way back. There were a lot of people there that day. Becca had been allowed to bring a friend. Normally she would have been swimming with Dan, but she and her friend were too cool to be seen with him—her words, not mine."

"I'm sorry, Sienna."

"I am, too. I remember when it happened. I'd been whining. Mom was mad at me. Dad had his eyes closed and was stretched out on a blanket. Becca and her friend wouldn't let me near them."

"And no one saw your brother struggling."

She shook her head. "My dad walked out on us two months later. I haven't seen him since. Mom fell apart. She kept a roof over our head, but she was never the same. She left right before I was supposed to start high school. That's why I came here to live with Grammy. Becca and Aaron had been stationed overseas at the time. When they returned, I moved in with them. I haven't seen my mother in years."

"Wait. Back up. Your mom left you? You were a freshman when you moved here. I remember."

"I do, too." She couldn't help but smile. The instant she stepped foot in Sunrise Bend, she'd fallen in love with it. "When I realized Mom wasn't coming back, I called Becca, Becca called our grandmother and it was settled. I'd stay with her until Becca, Aaron and baby Connor returned to the states."

"I can see why you're close to your sister."

"Yeah. She's always looked out for me. We had each other when we didn't have anyone else. Still do."

"That's how it is with my family, too." He veered to the left to follow the kids. "We're always here for each other."

"I know. I think it's amazing. It's been—" she hesitated, unsure of how to say what was on her heart "—eye-opening for me in some ways. This is how a family is supposed to work. No matter how hard Becca and I try to give Connor and Lily—and soon, my baby—a family they can count on, it's always in the backs of our minds it could fall apart. That someone will just walk away."

"I know what you mean." He stared ahead.

"You do?" She couldn't imagine he had any idea what she meant, not after she'd spent these wonderful weeks with his loving mom, his dad, who was more than willing to drop anything for his family at a moment's notice, his sisters and brother—they were tight. None of them were walking away from this family. Why would they?

"Did Erica ever mention our little brother, Cody, to you?"

She knew Cody had died in a car accident a few years ago, and Holly had been married to him at the time. Then Holly and Clara had moved here, where she'd promptly fallen in love with Jet. "I know the basics, but she doesn't talk about him."

"When he was a teenager, he made some poor choices. Got in with the wrong crowd." His jaw clenched. "Long story short, a few years after he graduated, his actions were affecting us all. We had to put a horse down because of him, and a lot of stuff was said. By all of us."

She scrunched her nose, dreading hearing the rest.

"He took off. Cut us out of his life." The tension seemed to drain from him, leaving resignation in its wake. "You know Holly was married to him, right?"

"Yes. And Clara is his baby."

"Yeah, well, none of us knew he'd gotten married. And Holly didn't even know he had a family. He told her he was an only child. An orphan."

"Oh, Blaine. I'm so, so sorry." Sienna reached over and placed her hand on his bicep. It flexed beneath her fingers. She withdrew her hand. "He died before you two could make things right."

He nodded, then gave her an anguished glance. "I tried. I called him. Texted him. He never answered. And part of it was my fault."

"Why do you say that?"

"I could have stopped him from hanging out with those guys when he was younger. I could have—"

"No, you couldn't have." She shook her head rapidly before shifting to study him. "We make our own choices. Don't blame yourself."

He flicked a closed-off glance her way. "You don't understand."

"I do understand." Boy, did she. How many times over the years had she watched each member of her family grapple with guilt and blame over her brother's death? "I used to think I could have saved my brother, too."

"That's different."

"Maybe. But I carried it for a long time. If only I hadn't been whining, my mom would have seen him. That sort of thing. I think my sister still thinks it was her fault.

It's probably why she struggles with anxiety and can't see straight when it comes to Aaron. Both of my parents blamed themselves. It was in their every move, every silence. I think we all have an alternate version of what should have happened that day at the reservoir—if only we'd done things differently."

He didn't respond.

"What would you have done differently?" She asked it quietly, holding her breath to see if he would answer.

Seconds stretched in silence, until finally he glanced her way. "I wouldn't have kept his secrets. I would have told my dad the day it all started. Then Cody would have stayed away from those guys, he would have had a good life—here, with us."

Sienna closed her eyes briefly. *Oh, Blaine.* She wanted to comfort him. Wanted to share some hard truths with him. But she could feel the mood, and after years of dealing with her sister, her nephew, her niece and, yes, even her ex-husband, she'd learned when to keep her mouth shut.

Instead, she did the only thing she could. She prayed.

Oh, merciful Lord, please heal Blaine's wounds from his brother's death. Help him release the guilt he holds, and show him the truth. That he's loved by You. That he's forgiven.

"Blaine?"

"Hmm?" It looked like he was battling powerful emotions.

"Have you ever asked God to forgive you? You know, for keeping Cody's secrets?"

Pressing his lips together, he nodded.

"Then let the guilt go. You're forgiven."

He didn't say another word, and a few minutes later,

Connor and Lily parked their four-wheelers near a dry creek bed along a line of trees. Blaine parked, too, and as Sienna reached for the door handle, he placed his hand on her arm.

"Wait."

She blinked, watching him.

"Thank you." So much tension, so much emotion, trembled in the words. "I needed to hear that."

"We can't change the past." She covered his hand with her own. "But we can do things differently in the future."

We can't change the past. An hour later, Blaine still couldn't get her words out of his head. They'd eaten the sandwiches, potato salad, chips and cookies Sienna had packed, and now Connor and Lily were helping clean everything up. Lily was chattering about how fun it was riding out here but she missed the puppies. Sienna stood off to the side with her hands against her lower back as she attempted to stretch.

He couldn't tear his gaze away. She was beautiful. Loose waves of red hair were pulled back into a ponytail, and her dress revealed her toned arms and baby bump. She looked over her shoulder at him and offered a soft smile. It slammed him in the chest.

He felt it all the way to his core.

All the questions about him and marriage and being a father melted away. He could see himself with her, gladly raising her baby as his own.

Too bad it would never work.

His priority was the ranch. Her priorities were her sister, nephew and niece.

He was manual labor. She was intellectual.

He lived in Sunrise Bend. She lived in Casper.

He was never anyone's first choice. She was his first choice and had been since he'd met her.

"Blaine?" Connor was in front of him. "Would it be alright if Lily and I headed back now? I know the way. I want to show her where we saw the prairie dogs."

"It's fine with me, but you'll have to ask your aunt."

Sienna's smile broadened. "Go ahead. Be careful, though. Don't go too fast."

Blaine wanted to chuckle. Four-wheelers were meant to go fast, and these were teenagers they were talking about. He glanced at Lily, and a wave of protectiveness came over him. Maybe Sienna was right to caution them. He'd hate to see either of them hurt.

"We won't." Lily grabbed her helmet as Connor quickly shut the lid on the cooler and carried it to the bed of the truck. Then they started the four-wheelers, revved them a few times and took off toward the sloping land in the distance.

"Want to follow them?" Blaine lifted the quilt and carefully folded it before tucking it under his arm.

"We can give them a head start."

Good, because he needed to talk to her privately. Normally, he would keep his thoughts to himself. But having her only a few feet away and it being just the two of them loosened his tongue.

"Sienna, do you ever miss living here?"

"All the time." She turned back to him. A breeze tickled stray hair around her face. "I loved living here."

Hope spread through him. If she loved living here once, maybe she'd be interested in living here again.

"It's been—" he tried to find the right words "—great having you back." *Great? Try amazing, life-changing.* He wasn't good at this.

"I've enjoyed it, too." Her eyes glowed in appreciation, making him bolder.

"Back in high school, I had a thing for you."

"You did?"

She had to have known, hadn't she? He nodded. "I did."

"I didn't realize…" Her eyebrows drew together as she tilted her head. "You were easy to be with. There was no drama. I could just be me."

Was that a good thing? The way she was looking at him made him think it was. He closed the short distance between them.

"I might still have a thing for you." His skin prickled. What if she rejected him?

"I might have one for you, too."

Hope ran rampant through his veins. He caressed her shoulders, running his hands down her biceps to her hands. Then he slid his hands around her waist. Her stomach prevented him from getting too close. It reminded him that she was carrying a precious baby inside her.

Blaine had spent his entire life caring for newborn animals, helping them grow, keeping them safe, protecting their mothers. They were his responsibility and he considered it a privilege.

"Where do you live, Sienna?" He leaned in closer, wanting to hear every detail of her life. "A house? Apartment?"

She looked surprised, but she melted in his arms. "Apartment. We sold the house after the divorce."

"What's it like?"

"I don't know." She smiled up at him, gently biting the corner of her bottom lip. "I just kind of live there. I didn't have the heart to do much with it. I do know one thing that's missing, though—a cat. My ex was allergic, but I always wanted a kitty to spoil."

"A cat, huh? Is that the only thing?" He was so close his lips were almost touching hers. With one hand on her lower back, he caressed her cheek with the back of his index finger.

He heard her sharp intake of breath and knew he was affecting her as much as she was him.

Slowly, he lowered his mouth to hers. The kiss was everything he'd imagined. The feel of her in his arms—so soft—brought out the protector in him. The one that had ached to be hers since he'd first met her.

He pressed her closer, and his pulse raced as her hands crept behind his neck and she kissed him back. Having her in his arms felt right. He couldn't imagine not having her in them forever.

Slowly, they broke away, and her shimmering gaze locked with his as she placed her hand against his cheek.

"You make me feel cherished."

"That's how you're supposed to feel." He continued holding her. "You're special, Sienna."

Her eyelashes dipped. Had he said the wrong thing?

"Come on. We'd better catch up with the kids." She took his hand and led him toward the truck. He opened the passenger door for her and lifted her by the waist into the seat. Her cheeks flushed, and he almost leaned in to kiss her again.

Instead, he shut the door and jogged around to the driver's side.

Did he dare hope that a future with Sienna might not be as out of the question as he'd thought?

Chapter Ten

A future with Blaine was out of the question. He was temptation wrapped in chaps and a cowboy hat, and it was all Sienna could do not to cry as she thought about returning to Casper for good in less than a week.

It had been two weeks since the picnic.

Two weeks since her knees turned to jelly at Blaine's kiss.

Two weeks of magnetic glances, of suppers together, of playing with the puppies and talking about the little stuff. Favorite movies, the best flavor of ice cream—mint chocolate chip, of course—how they got through boring winter nights. She loved to read cozy mysteries and watch cooking shows in the winter. He liked watching football.

Two weeks of helping Blaine find homes for all the puppies, except for Sushi. Two weeks of Connor hanging out with his new friends—bonfires, ice-cream runs and all the fun she and Blaine had hoped he'd have.

Two weeks of learning the ins and outs of candle making, as Reagan and Julie taught her more each day. She found it challenging, invigorating.

At least it was a gorgeous Saturday. Sienna sat in the rocking chair on the cabin's porch, waiting for Mac to pick up Connor and Lily so they could ride horses with Kaylee and her friends at his ranch. Blaine's friends were incredibly thoughtful. They treated her and her niece and nephew as if they were family. What she wouldn't give to be part of their group permanently.

How was she going to leave all this?

Even Becca and Aaron seemed on the verge of reuniting for good. The hope in Becca's voice every night when she talked to her filled Sienna with joy. Maybe her sister would get back to the loving mom she'd been before their marriage began unraveling.

Sienna sighed. Where did that leave her, though?

Troy had texted her a few days ago to tell her she was being selfish. Ironic, coming from him. She'd called him back, but he hadn't answered. She still couldn't make up her mind on what to do about his upcoming court petition, and since he wouldn't be filing it until after the baby was born, she wasn't in a rush to decide.

The reality of the baby coming soon was getting harder to ignore, though. She'd had a routine prenatal checkup last week. Everything looked good. When she returned to Casper, she'd start having weekly appointments. It didn't seem possible the baby would be arriving so soon.

Mac's truck rolled up, stopping in front of the cabin. She pressed her hands into the arms of the rocking chair and hefted herself to a standing position.

Opening the cabin door, she called, "Connor, Lily— Mac and Kaylee are here."

Lily, wearing her new cowboy boots they'd purchased last week, raced out in shorts and a T-shirt, her hair in a French braid. Connor took a little longer, but when he appeared, Sienna couldn't help but smile. Her nephew was growing up. His black T-shirt no longer hung limp on his frame. He'd developed muscles from all the ranch work. He had on jeans, cowboy boots and a cowboy hat. He looked the part of a ranch hand, that was for sure.

"Okay, guys, remember what we talked about." She followed them down the porch steps.

"Don't worry. I'll text you when I get there, Aunt Sienna." Lily waved goodbye.

"I'll make sure Lil's safe," Connor said. "She's ridden before, but I have more experience."

"I know you will. And answer the phone if your mom calls." They nodded, waved and loaded into the truck. Soon it was disappearing in a cloud of dust.

Leaving her alone.

One thing she hadn't missed in the weeks she'd spent here was being alone.

Come Thursday, she'd be on her own in Casper again. Alone in her apartment. Alone at night. Alone until her baby was born. Sure, Becca and the kids lived nearby, but it wasn't the same.

Sienna trudged up the steps and reclaimed the rocking chair. She'd never minded being alone. But lately... She glanced at Blaine's house. She craved his companionship. Liked being around him. He made her feel like she was the only woman in the world. She loved it, really.

Sighing, she closed her eyes.

There was no future for them. They lived hours apart. And she had to get used to that reality.

"Hey, did they ditch you?"

Her eyes opened at the sound of Blaine's voice, and her lips curved upward. "Yes."

"What do you say we head into town for some ice cream?" He arched his eyebrows, propping his boot on the bottom porch step. Those blue eyes drew her in, making her want things she had no right wanting.

"Make it an iced decaf coffee from Brewed Awakening, and I'm in."

He grinned. "Done."

The drive into town did nothing to ease the tightening in her chest at having to leave in a few days. Even Blaine's chatter about grazing the cattle on the far edges of his property didn't cheer her up, and normally she loved hearing him talk about the ranch.

After parking, they went into the coffee shop and exchanged chitchat with Joe, Bridget's elderly employee, for a few minutes before ordering iced coffees and muffins. Then they took their drinks to the table near the front window.

Her mind flashed back to the day she arrived and stumbled onto this place. All the snapshots in her head of her and the baby rushed back. New pictures clicked by, one by one, and this time, they all included Blaine.

Him holding the baby. Pushing a stroller next to her. Carrying her toddler inside.

She pulled back her shoulders, taking a deep breath.

"Is everything okay?" He frowned, dunking his straw into his drink.

"Yeah." She tried to reassure him with a smile.

"The kids are fine at Mac's. I'd trust him with my life." He reached over and covered her hand.

"That's not it." She blinked rapidly. "It's going to be hard to leave all this."

His gaze sharpened. "Then don't."

"I have to."

She wasn't sure if his silence reassured her or made it worse. He seemed to be grappling with something.

"Why don't I skip tomorrow night?" His eyes seared into hers. The guys were all meeting tomorrow night at Randy's to go over what needed to be done for Randy and Hannah's wedding. Apparently, they were grilling fresh trout. No women were allowed. "He'll understand."

"No, that wouldn't be right." Sienna wouldn't take that from him. "He's your best friend. You need to be there."

This conversation suddenly felt heavy. Too heavy.

"Becca shared some good news with me last night." There. It was easier to talk about her sister. "It sounds like Aaron is moving back in before the kids return. I want that for them."

He averted his eyes. "Yeah, I do, too."

"It will be nice to get back to my weekly coffee dates with Erica." She ignored the way her throat tightened. Erica had driven to the ranch last weekend, and Sienna had enjoyed catching up with her about all the drama back in Casper. They'd swapped tales of pregnancy woes, the most recent being the fact Sienna could no longer see her toes when she stood.

"Sounds like you miss Casper." A muscle in his cheek flexed.

Did she? She stared out the window at the pretty purple and pink flowers in window boxes across the street. "I suppose I miss what it was. It won't be the same when I go back."

"What do you mean?" He looked puzzled.

"Oh, you know. Things like taking Connor and Lily to my house for a movie and a sleepover so Becca and Aaron could have date night. We did that a lot when the kids were little. I know all the Disney cartoons by heart. But they're older now. They don't need a babysitter. Things have changed."

He smiled.

She shifted the ice with her straw. "I'll have to figure out how to manage the baby and working. There's a day care nearby, but it makes me nervous. Don't get me wrong, I like my job. It gets repetitive sometimes and I get frustrated when we aren't awarded the grants we apply for, but my coworkers are nice and the hours are good."

"What else?"

"Nothing, I guess." She shrugged. "Everything else will be the same. My apartment, the café where I buy soup and salad every Wednesday, coffee dates with your sister, going to my church." Instead of cheering her up, the thoughts of returning to her routine gave her a case of the blues. "You've lived here your entire life, haven't you?"

He nodded.

"What would you miss if you moved away?"

"Me, move?" he scoffed. "Not happening."

"Well, I know that." She refrained from shaking her head. "Hypothetically speaking."

His eyebrows dipped into a *V*. "Well... I'd miss everything, I guess. My family and friends, for sure. I'd miss saddling up Boots and riding to all the hidden places on my ranch where no one would ever think to go. There are a few spots in the spring with the prettiest wildflowers. I like big, open spaces. No crowds. No one around at all for miles. It would be tough to give all that up."

Yes, it would be tough. She returned her attention to her coffee. She couldn't picture him in a city. He belonged on the prairie, in his house on the ranch. Near his family. Near his friends. Doing what he did best— taking care of what was his.

So why did she have the most irrational desire that *she* could be his? Was that why she asked him the question? Hoping he'd express even a hint of dissatisfaction with his life? A longing to experience life somewhere else? Somewhere like Casper?

Foolish thinking. He would never give up his ranch, and she'd never ask him to. It was a part of him. Something he couldn't and wouldn't turn his back on.

Just like Becca and the kids were part of her. She couldn't and wouldn't turn her back on them, either.

And that left them both exactly where they were. Together for a few more days. And then this romance would be over.

"Something wrong?" Randy, holding a can of soda, strolled over to Blaine the following evening. Ned came over as well, then sprawled out on the lawn to lick his paws.

All the guys had arrived an hour ago. Jet and Mac were grilling the trout, Sawyer and Austin were discussing the dry conditions, and Blaine was doing what he did best. Standing there silently, taking it all in.

"What?" Blaine asked, startled. "Nothing's wrong."

Everything was wrong.

Sienna was leaving Thursday, only four days from now—not that he was counting—and she'd made it clear yesterday at the coffee shop she was going back to Casper. For her, there were no other alternatives.

When she'd mentioned it being hard to leave, hope had flared so bright, it blinded his good sense, only to be snuffed out as the conversation progressed. And then she'd asked what he'd miss if he ever moved away from Sunrise Bend.

He'd never once considered leaving.

And just talking about it yesterday confirmed he wasn't going anywhere. Sunrise Bend was his home. The ranch was more than a job—it was his life.

"Are you sure?" Randy asked. "You're not mad at me for not keeping my end of the bargain, are you?"

"What are you talking about?" Blaine sifted through his brain to try to figure out what Randy was referring to. Nope. Nothing.

"I always said I wasn't getting married." A corner of his mouth quirked up as his eyes twinkled. "And look at me. On the verge of forever with Hannah."

"Oh, that." Blaine grinned. "Of course I'm mad at you. We were all going to be bachelors. And now it's down to me and your brother—your much smarter brother, I might add."

"I don't know. Snatching up Hannah seemed pretty smart to me."

"Yeah, I don't blame you." Blaine playfully punched Randy's upper arm. "She's perfect for you, man."

"I can't wait until the wedding's over."

"The planning getting to you?"

"You can't imagine. Miss Patty has been waiting for this moment for years. Years. I mean, I love Hannah's mom. And it's nice to know she loves me, too. But she and Hannah are poring over things I just don't care about. Like give me a catalog of fishing lures and I'll spend hours on it. But place settings and cake flavors?" He shook his head as if disgusted. "I can't do it much longer."

"You won't have to. In a few short weeks, the wedding will be over. You two can go on your honeymoon, and get started on your new life together."

"Thanks, man." Randy blew out a loud breath. "I needed to hear that."

"Can I ask you a question? A personal one?" Blaine hesitated before continuing. "How did you know Hannah was the one?"

Randy got a faraway look in his eyes. "The exact moment? I don't know. It kind of crept up on me. But when she made me keep Ned overnight before she knew about my heart condition, I realized how perceptive and caring she was. And I couldn't imagine not having her with me or, worse, watching someone else fall in love with her. I was scared, though, and I didn't act on it."

"What made you act?"

"Passing out in the store before Sawyer's wedding rehearsal. Kind of forced me to tell her the truth. And all of you, too. I spent the sorriest night of my life that night trying to convince myself I couldn't have her, that it wasn't fair to her."

Blaine didn't speak. He'd never heard Randy talk like this. He hadn't known he'd gone through all this.

"But the big lug over there talked sense into me." Randy chuckled, gesturing to Austin, who gave them a wary glance. "Made me see I was being dumb."

"That's what brothers are for." Jet came over and put his arm around Blaine's neck, ruffling his hair. "Right, Blaine?"

"If you say so."

The other guys joined them.

"What are big brothers for?" Austin asked.

"Telling us we're being idiots about women." Randy grinned.

"Ahh." Austin nodded. "I couldn't let you turn your back on Hannah. You two were meant for each other."

Blaine wanted to back up a step, to get out of this circle of teasing and truths, but he stayed where he was.

Randy hitched his chin to Mac. "How did you know Bridget was the one?"

"Easy. She was getting the coffee shop ready to open, and she and I discussed hiring Kaylee part-time. I offered her a discount on rent if she'd hire Kaylee, and do you know what she said to me?"

They all shook their heads.

"To keep my discount. She said other things, too. Put it this way, boys, she was not impressed by me. At all." He lifted one shoulder in a shrug. "And that, my friends, got my attention. But it wasn't until I spent time with her that I realized how much I needed her. She's direct, kind and, well, pretty blunt."

"I could have told you that." Sawyer lifted his hands as if to say *duh*. Bridget and Sawyer had been friends for years in New York City, and Sawyer still referred to her as being like a sister to him.

"What about you and Holly, Jet?" Randy asked.

Jet flushed, scratching the toe of his athletic shoe over the ground. "I don't know. It was really complicated. And I fought it. Hard."

Blaine tilted his head to watch his brother more carefully. Last year when Holly moved to the ranch, they'd talked about her, but Jet had been closed off about his feelings. Blaine had picked up on the fact that Jet liked her and had encouraged him to not let her get away.

"Complicated?" Austin teased in a nonthreatening way. "She was your dead brother's wife. And she had his baby. I'd say it was complicated."

Jet chuckled, shaking his head. "Yeah, well, what can I say? I do everything the hard way."

They all joined in laughing. Then, for some weird reason, all eyes turned to him.

"So Sienna…" Mac arched his eyebrows. "What's going on there?"

"Nothing," Blaine snapped. "She and the kids are leaving Thursday."

He didn't miss the sly glances they all exchanged. It irritated him.

"Are you hung up on the idea of her having a baby?" Austin asked.

"No." He wasn't, either.

"Well, if you don't think you could raise another man's child…" Austin's voice trailed off. "Your brother's doing a good job."

"That's not an issue." He widened his stance, crossing his arms over his chest.

"She seems into you," Jet said. Then he frowned. "But what do I know?"

He inhaled sharply, wanting to tell all of these idiots to mind their own business.

"Look, I'm not getting married," Blaine said. "You all can have your weddings and whatnots, but at the end of the day, it's just going to be me and my ranch." He tightened his jaw, hating the words because they were no longer true. He didn't mean them the way he used to.

He wanted Sienna on the ranch with him.

Wanted the wedding and the whatnot.

Wanted it all.

"Come on, guys." Jet made the settle-down motion with his hands. "Sienna's only a few months out from a divorce, and she's having a baby. She's probably not ready to think about dating."

Exactly. Disappointment plunged deep within him, though. Jet had spoken the truth, so why was Blaine still thinking about forever?

"Uh, Mac, is the trout on fire?" Jet pointed to the grill.

"Oh, no!" He jogged over to it, flames rising, the rest of the guys joining him.

"Hey, don't listen to those guys." Jet came up to stand next to Blaine. "If you want to stay single, it's fine by me."

He probably should appreciate his brother's words, but they rubbed him the wrong way. He didn't want to stay single. But he didn't want to hash it all out here, either. Or anywhere, really.

Why couldn't relationships be easy? Why couldn't he just tell Sienna how he felt about her? And why couldn't she jump in his arms and tell him she felt the same?

He wanted her to stay. What did Casper have that he didn't?

Connor and Lily. And Becca. And her job.

Right.

Austin's phone rang, and as he answered it, Blaine turned his attention back to Jet. "I don't know what I want."

"Really?" Jet looked surprised. "You?"

"What's that supposed to mean?"

"I don't know." He shrugged. "It's just that you're steady. You seem to know what's right for you. I can always count on you. I didn't realize you were having second thoughts about staying single. Does Sienna feel the same?"

Blaine often felt like the less competent brother when

he was around Jet. To hear his brother say he could always count on him meant a lot.

"I don't know, and it doesn't matter. Her life's in Casper."

Austin's voice rang out loudly. "I've got to go. Cassie's grandfather is in the hospital. I'm meeting her and her mom there." He pointed to Randy. "The babysitter has AJ until nine. If I'm not back by then, will you go over there and watch him for me?"

"Of course, man." Randy gave Austin a quick hug. "Tell Cassie we're praying."

"I will." He took long strides to the side of the house, then disappeared.

"Alright, who's ready to talk about the bachelor party?" Mac asked.

"Me." Blaine raised his hand. Anything to get his mind off Sienna.

"Sienna, can I talk to you a minute?"

Sienna looked up from her desk Monday afternoon as she was putting the final touches on a package. Julie was standing nearby.

Holly had taken a sniffly Clara home at lunch and was taking the rest of the day off. Reagan was in the back making more candles. And Lily was spending her remaining afternoons at Blaine's, watching the puppies with his dad. Sienna wasn't fighting her on the issue anymore. It didn't matter in the grand scheme of things.

"Of course." Sienna wiped her hands down the sides of her shorts and gave Julie her full attention.

"We sure have enjoyed having you and the kids—although I'm sure they wouldn't want to hear me call them kids—here this summer." Her warm smile sparked Sienna's emotions, bringing the sting of tears to the backs of her eyes. She was really struggling with the thought of leaving this generous family.

"We've enjoyed it, too." Sienna attempted to smile. "You made us feel very welcome."

"That's partly what I wanted to talk to you about."

A twinge of worry made Sienna pause. She sounded way too serious.

Julie dragged over a nearby chair to face Sienna, then took a seat. "That's better. My feet and my back ache this time of the day."

"Mine, too." Boy, did she know it.

"I know you have your own life back in Casper. A good job, family. Friends, my daughter included. I'm thankful you and Erica have each other. So forgive me for asking this, but I'd hate for you to leave without me even trying."

Sienna drew her eyebrows together, confused.

"Would you consider working with us permanently?"

She blinked repeatedly, not expecting those words to come out of Julie's mouth.

"Um…" How could she possibly respond? Julie was right. In Casper, she did have a life, a job, a family. She enjoyed her weekly coffee dates with Erica.

But Casper didn't have Blaine.

"I can see I surprised you." Julie took off her glasses and rubbed the lenses with a tissue. "Don't worry about answering right away. I know how close you are to your sister and Connor and Lily. I get it, hon, I do. But you took to the candle-making process so quickly. Reagan and I have a hard time keeping up with the demand. You're a natural at it. And we like working with you. In fact, we'd like to see a whole lot more of you."

They wanted her around.

They thought she was good at making candles.

They liked her.

After too many years of worrying about everyone else's happiness, it was as jolting as a jug of ice water poured over her head to have someone thinking about her happiness for a change.

But, as nice as the offer was, there was no way she could accept. The reasons tapped out, rapid-fire.

She needed to be near Becca and the kids.

She was about to have a baby.

She wouldn't be able to work for a few months once it was born.

Oh, and then there was the itty-bitty problem of Julie's son.

Blaine tempted her to stay. Even more than the charm of Sunrise Bend, the joy of working with these kind, fun women. She wanted to be near him. Didn't want this romance to end.

"If things were different—" she swallowed, trying to find the right words "—I would seriously consider it."

Hope lit Julie's face. "We'd pay you a good salary. And we can offer benefits, thanks to Tess's research. She's more than a bookkeeper, let me tell you."

"Yes, I know." She didn't want to hurt Julie's feelings, but she couldn't let the woman think for a minute she could stay. "But like you said, I have my sister to consider."

"I understand." Julie tried to hide her disappointment as she nodded. "I had to try, though. You're like family. In fact, I was hoping for a while there you might become family."

Her back stiffened. "What do you mean?"

"Well, with you and Blaine getting along so well."

She didn't know what to say, so she remained silent.

"Blaine is—" Julie paused, glancing at her hands before returning her attention to Sienna "—not the easiest to read if you don't know him well."

She'd always found him easy to read. Like a large-print book with a light shining on it.

"Oh, I know my son looks like he's taking life in stride. But there are depths to him he doesn't talk about. He keeps things close to his heart."

Sienna supposed it was true. But didn't most people?

"But I know my Blaine." She pushed her glasses up the bridge of her nose. "And I know you're good for him. Just like I know he's good for you."

She opened her mouth to protest, but Julie held out her hand. "Before you say anything, hear me out. Maybe the timing's wrong. I know divorce is worse than a death in some ways, and it takes time to process. Then there's the baby. I can't begin to imagine what you're going through."

Sienna held her breath as her throat tightened. Her divorce had been like a death. But it hadn't been sudden or shocking. She'd felt it coming, had known their marriage was sinking for a long time.

The end had still been painful, though.

"Whether you know it or not, my son needed you and Connor and Lily this summer." Julie's tenderness was going to make her cry.

"We had fun with the puppies."

"It was more than the puppies. You helped him loosen up. He's had tunnel vision when it comes to the ranch, especially the hay and that pasture. I told him he can't control the weather—only God can—but it went in one ear and out the other. If you hadn't been around, he would still be beating himself up over it. Instead, he's been out and about this summer with you and the kids. It's done him a world of good. He's almost back to himself."

Back to himself. Yeah, she could see that. "He mentioned Cody."

"Good." She nodded. "He doesn't open up about him. Keeps the hurt all jammed down inside." Julie clasped her hands. "I think we all blamed ourselves for Cody cutting us out of his life. I know I did. The worst was not knowing he'd gotten married until after he died. Those regrets are always there, even as life goes on. His father and I didn't handle Cody right, didn't know how to stop him from self-destructing when he was in high school. I'm sure each of us, including Blaine, has a list of things we would have done differently."

Sienna knew it to be true. When her dad walked out, it had crushed her and Becca and their mother. And years later when her mom left without so much as a goodbye, Sienna had been crushed all over again, but this time she hadn't been all that surprised.

People left. With no warning. No explanation.

The people she'd needed, the ones she'd depended on, had abandoned her. Maybe that was why she'd never allowed herself to depend on Troy too much. Maybe she'd chosen a husband who wouldn't be around. It had been easier that way.

"Anyway, enough with the depressing talk. Thank you for bringing my boy's cheerful nature back." Julie patted her hand. "I've missed it."

"I don't think I'm the one to thank."

"Oh, you are. You two were friends long ago, and look at you now. Friends again. Forgive a meddling mom for hoping it could be more. I want you to know you are always welcome here."

"You're not meddling, but thank you." The tears she'd been holding back were knocking at the door. The Mayer family had treated her like one of their own. What she wouldn't give to have them in her life permanently.

But Blaine wasn't hers. This ranch wasn't Casper. And she wasn't taking risks with love.

The people she'd needed might have walked away from her, but she would never abandon Becca, Connor or Lily. She'd be by their sides, whatever the cost.

Chapter Eleven

He'd let his brother walk out of his life. Could he really let Sienna walk out, too?

Blaine brushed Boots after checking cattle Wednesday morning. Everything on the ranch was going smoothly. The bulls were happy to be with the cows. He and Jim were negotiating with suppliers to buy additional feed for the winter. And he'd been checking off his never-ending hot list item by item each day. He was even close to making a decision about keeping Tiara and Ollie. But all he could think about was the beautiful redhead who'd stolen his heart as a teen and held it in her hands as an adult.

She and the kids were leaving tomorrow around noon. Yesterday had been her final day working at the candle shop.

Why was it so hard to think about her leaving?

He set aside the brush and began picking the horse's hooves. A few stones were dislodged from the front left. He expertly made his way around to the other hooves.

Blaine had spent every evening with Sienna this week. They'd held hands on the bench swing in his backyard and watched the stars come out while Connor and Lily played with the puppies. They'd talked about their fears and their dreams, tiptoeing around their feelings for each other, but those feelings had been there, shimmering between them.

He hadn't told her he didn't want her to go. Hadn't admitted she'd be taking his heart with him.

This ranch wouldn't be the same without her. Would he still love it the way he did before she'd arrived? Or would it feel empty? Meaningless?

Was he emotionally prepared to find out?

Connor strode through the stables with Ollie trotting by his side. Good, a distraction.

"What's up, Connor?"

"I was wondering about something." The kid had on his worried face, and Blaine hadn't seen it in a few weeks. He hoped this didn't involve Connor's mother.

"Yeah?" He guided Boots toward the paddock leading to the pasture where he kept the horses. Connor and Ollie fell in beside him.

"Have you decided if you're keeping Tiara and Ollie yet?"

"I want to." He squinted at the horses grazing in the distance. "I'm not sure how I'll make it work by myself, though. Your sister really helped me out all summer."

"I've been thinking. If you kept the dogs, you could hire someone like Lily when they have puppies. You know, like hiring a babysitter. For the first couple of weeks at least."

"That's not a bad idea." It grew on him as he considered it. "Especially in the summer. I'm not sure about the rest of the year with school and all."

"Well, how often do you need to breed them? If they had one litter each summer, would it be enough?"

They came to the gate, and Blaine opened it, patting the horse's neck before letting him loose. The sunny day would get hot later, but for now it was peaceful and mild. Then he closed the gate again and turned to Connor.

"Now that you mention it, I don't see a problem with breeding once a year. I'll run it by Laura. See what she thinks."

Blaine wanted to keep the dogs. As soon as the puppies went to their new homes two weeks from now, he planned on bringing Tiara around the ranch more, too. To only breed them once a year would take a lot of the worries off his mind.

"So you'll keep Ollie?" Connor's eyes lit with hope.

"If Laura agrees to one litter a year? Yes."

He nodded eagerly and let out a loud sigh in relief.

"You love Ollie, don't you?" Blaine gestured for him to join him as he walked down the lane toward the equipment shed.

Connor nodded. "He's a good dog."

"He is." Blaine paused, shifting to face him. "I have to keep him and Tiara together. You know that, right?"

"I wouldn't want them separated."

"I talked to your aunt about this, and I don't want to get your hopes up, but if your mom and dad don't mind, I'd like for you and your sister to have Sushi."

"Really?" His eyes popped. "Lily is going to flip. That would be awesome."

"Yeah, well, don't tell her yet. I don't want her disappointed if your parents say no."

"Could we take him with us when we go home tomorrow?" Connor asked.

"No, he's not ready to leave his mama yet. I can drive him down in a week or two."

"You'd do that?"

"Yeah." Heat climbed his neck. Was he using the puppy as an excuse to see Sienna again? Maybe. Maybe not. He wanted the kids to have the pup.

"Is your sister up?"

"She was eating a bowl of cereal before I came out here."

"Would you do me a favor and bring her to my ranch office? I have something for each of you."

Connor gave him a quizzical look, nodded and jogged away. Blaine lengthened his strides and went into the pole barn, where his office was located. Inside the office, he opened the bottom drawer of his desk and pulled out the envelopes he'd prepared.

Both kids had helped him out all summer. He'd paid Connor an hourly wage each week, and he'd given Sienna money every Friday to give to Lily for watching the pups. But he wanted to give them something more—a bonus for making his work easy these past two months.

A few minutes later, the teens arrived, rosy-cheeked and short of breath. They sat on the folding chairs opposite his desk. He leaned his forearms on it.

"You both stepped up and helped me out this summer big-time," Blaine said. Connor and Lily exchanged confused glances. He continued. "Connor, you took to ranching like a pro. With you and Bryce taking care of the chores, Jim and I were able to get the hay cut and baled before it dried out too much. That can be the difference between the cattle having enough to eat in the winter or not. I needed you, and you came through for me."

"I liked being out there, Blaine."

He smiled at him, then turned his attention to Lily. "And Lily, without your help, I don't know how I would have taken care of the puppies. You have the touch with animals."

He tapped both envelopes on the desk then handed one to Lily and the other to Connor. "This is a bonus. For all your help. I appreciate it. Don't open it here. You'll just embarrass me."

"Thank you." Lily's eyes shimmered and she stood and gave Blaine a quick hug. "Thanks for letting me help with the puppies. I'll never forget it."

"Yeah, thanks." Connor nodded, his smile shy. "I won't forget all you taught me about the ranch, either."

"You're welcome. Now go on and enjoy your day." He waved them off, grinning to himself as they whispered to each other all the way outside.

He sat there for a long time, his thoughts turning to his friends, how each of them had taken a chance on love. Could he do the same?

Sienna liked him. It was obvious. But love? He didn't know if she loved him.

Well, she didn't have to love him yet.

If she'd consider staying here in Sunrise Bend, they could explore their feelings more. Maybe she'd learn to love him. All he had to do was ask her to stay.

Sienna's spirits faded that afternoon as she placed her neatly folded clothes into a suitcase. This was it. The last hurrah. Their final full day here.

Connor and Lily had burst into the cabin earlier all excited about the cash bonus Blaine had given each of them. And an hour later, Julie had picked them up and taken them to the candle shop, where she'd planned a surprise going-away party for them with their new friends. Teens only—well, except for Julie and Kevin, who were in charge of the food and would be chaperoning the event.

Sienna had already cleaned out the fridge, packed

most of the snacks in a bin and thrown another load of towels into the washing machine. Tomorrow would be hard enough without having to do all the chores.

The closer her old life got, the bleaker it looked. She'd fallen hard for Blaine. And there was nothing she could do about it except leave. And hope her feelings for the cowboy would fade in time.

The buzz of her phone distracted her from packing. When she saw her sister's name, she immediately answered.

"Hey, Becca. What's going on?"

"Can you bring Connor and Lily home early?" Her sobs made her speech choppy, hard to understand. "Aaron left, and I don't think he's coming back."

Sienna stood there stunned as Becca cried.

"I tried everything, Sienna, I really did. I thought we were going to make it. But this morning he accused me of emotionally blackmailing him. I don't even know what that means." The crying commenced again, although it wasn't as raw this time. "He said I act like a martyr to punish him. I told him he's ridiculous. He slammed out of here."

Rubbing one eyebrow with her free hand, Sienna didn't even know where to start.

"I don't think he's coming back." The words were eerily quiet.

Danger signals blared in her mind as Sienna padded down the hall to the kitchen.

"You two have argued before," she said gently. "And you've spent the past two months together trying, Becca. He'll be back." When her sister didn't respond, her hands grew cold.

Sienna could handle crying. She could handle endless repetition of the same old complaints. But this—this silent pain—she recognized. Her mom had shut down the exact same way in the days before she walked out of her life for good. "Bec?"

"Just come home," she whispered. "I can't do this anymore."

Sienna didn't want to leave this afternoon. It was bad enough having to go tomorrow. And what would the kids say? They'd be upset. Lily was already struggling with leaving the puppies, and Connor had mentioned one final horseback ride tomorrow morning with Bryce.

But her sister's dead silence filled her with anxiety. Closing her eyes, she swayed slightly, trying to figure out what was best for everyone. She didn't know the severity of the situation.

Leaving today would mean losing out on her last night with Blaine. She couldn't do it.

"It's going to be okay, Becca." She gripped the phone tightly, doubting herself. "We'll be home tomorrow afternoon, and I'll stop and pick us up a pizza on the way in."

"No!" Her voice was haggard, sharp.

"It's only one night." Was she being selfish?

"Forget it." The words came out softly, despondently, like a vapor.

The call ended so abruptly, Sienna could only stare at the phone in her hand. After setting it on the counter, she pressed her fingers to her temples. Becca scared her when she was like this. Angry Becca, she could handle. But despondent Becca?

Sienna had lived with two despondent people who'd vanished from her life. What if her sister took off like their parents had? Would Sienna, Connor and Lily be returning to an empty house? With no sign of their mother?

She couldn't stand the thought of Connor and Lily being confused and hopeless and heartbroken.

The phone rang again, and she snatched it up. "Becca?"

"No, it's me." At the sound of Troy's voice, she recoiled. "I did what you wanted. Saw a doctor. Guess I really am a mental case. Hope you're happy."

His speech was stilted, odd. She'd dealt with this mood before, but for the life of her, she didn't know how to deal with it now.

"Anyhow, you got what you wanted. Now give me what I want."

She was aware of her sharp intake of breath as her chest tightened uncomfortably.

"I spoke with my lawyer," she said. "Regardless of what you think, I'm not happy that you suffer from a personality disorder, Troy. I wouldn't wish that on anyone."

"Then file the petition to have my rights waived. If you're the one who files it, I'll have a better chance of winning."

"It's so extreme. What if you change your mind a few years from now? You can't go back. You know that, right?"

"So is this about child support? We both know I'm not cut out to be a dad."

"It's not about child support." She pinched the bridge of her nose. "I don't want you doing something permanent you'll regret later."

"I won't regret it. I meant what I said. I want nothing to do with the kid. Nothing."

There was no sense arguing with him. It would go nowhere. But her heart still pounded.

If he wanted to cut all ties and all responsibilities, that was his decision, not hers. "I'm not filing the petition. If you want to, that's your choice. I certainly won't fight it. But I'm not helping you do this, either. Don't put this on me."

All the tension and worry from the past months spilled over as the line went dead. She widened her eyes at the phone in her hand.

She didn't have the time or mental space to think about Troy at the moment. Becca needed her. She was certain of it, and that meant her plans for leaving tomorrow were getting moved up to this afternoon.

Sienna would never forgive herself if she waited until tomorrow and came home to an empty house and her sister gone.

She pressed Becca's number and waited as it rang.

And rang. And rang.

She left a quick voice mail for her to call her back. Then she texted her, asking if she was okay.

No response.

She hurried to her bedroom and shoved all the remaining clothes from the dresser into her suitcases. Packed her makeup and toiletries.

And called Becca again.

No answer.

Dread churned inside her.

She was driving back as soon as the kids returned. She couldn't live with herself if she didn't.

Chapter Twelve

At the sound of a vehicle rumbling past the front of the house, Blaine hauled himself to a standing position in the spare room, keeping one of the puppies in the crook of his arm as he absentmindedly petted it. Connor and Lily must be back from the party his mom had put together.

The hours were speeding by too quickly. He hated the thought of Sienna leaving tomorrow.

That's why all afternoon, he'd been trying to figure out what to say to her tonight after supper. He needed to talk to her. Needed to ask her the hard question, the one she most likely would be saying no to.

But there was a chance she'd say yes. He had to at least try.

He was going to ask her to stay.

Mom already told him she'd asked Sienna to stay in Sunrise Bend and work for them. Sure, she'd declined, but if she changed her mind, she'd have a job here. And she could continue living in the cabin. A job and a place to live—two problems solved.

But he wasn't stupid. She didn't need a job or a place

to live. She needed to be near Connor and Lily and her sister. She'd said it time and again.

Still…he had to try. This was his life, too, and he wasn't imagining their connection. Maybe, just maybe, he'd be enough for her to stay.

It wasn't like she'd never see her loved ones again. In fact, she could go to Casper anytime she wanted. He'd drive her himself if need be. He would never rip her from her family.

Blaine set down the puppy and watched affectionately as it toddled off to Tiara. The roly-poly fluffballs had been fun to play with these past few weeks. He'd called Laura earlier, and she'd agreed one litter a year was reasonable and probably good for Tiara as well. As of today, the dogs were officially his.

A knock on the door made him jump. He slipped out of the room and strode down the hall to answer it.

Sienna was standing on his doorstep. Her eyes glimmered with worry and something else… Something he couldn't put his finger on.

"What's wrong?" He took her by the hand and led her inside. They made it to the living room before she turned to him. He waited for her to speak, but the silence grew, along with a sense of foreboding.

She bit her lower lip. "I feel terrible about this, but we're taking off early."

He looked into her worried green eyes, not sure he'd heard her correctly. "Come again?"

"Becca called. She wants us back tonight."

Just like that? He stiffened. "And you're going."

She nodded.

"Sienna, she'll be okay for one night." He wasn't sure how to handle this. How could he ask her to stay now?

He didn't want to have the conversation with her upset like this.

"I don't think so," she said quietly.

"Wait until tomorrow to leave. It won't even be twenty-four hours."

"I know, but…"

Was she wavering? He plunged ahead, antsy about the timing, but what else could he do? Let her leave without saying everything in his heart?

He'd done that with Cody. And he'd never seen his brother again.

"I was going to talk to you tonight, but while I have you alone…" He caressed her upper arms, but her tense muscles didn't relax. "I understand if you have to take the kids back to Casper. And I realize you have a lot going on there. But this summer—it's been incredible."

"It has been." Her eyes grew watery, and her voice was little more than a whisper.

"Honestly, I don't want it to end. Being with you, spending all this time with you, talking to you—I haven't been able to open up like this to a woman. Ever."

She gulped.

"I'm glad you're back in my life." He wished she would give him an indication—anything, really—that she wanted to hear what he was saying. "I had feelings for you in high school, and then you were gone. Now you're here, and my feelings never really went away."

She turned her head to the side, looking away from him.

"I get that this is bad timing with you being pregnant. And I know you have to return to Casper for the moment, but I want you to consider moving here. You can live in the cabin. You can work with Mom and Reagan and

Holly. I don't want what we have to end. We get along great. We're both mature, older now. We could date, keep getting to know each other until you're ready. I could see us together…forever."

A tear slipped out and dripped down her cheek as she looked up at him.

"Don't cry." He swiped away the tear with his thumb. "I don't want to make you cry."

A tender sob ripped from her throat, and she pressed her lips together, shaking her head.

"In my fantasies," she said, her voice wobbly, "I'd live in the cabin and work with your family, and you and I would date and get closer and be together forever." She attempted a smile, but it went horribly wrong. "But that's all it is, Blaine, a fantasy."

"It doesn't have to be." He drew her closer.

"I'm having a baby, Blaine." She took a step back, waving both hands to indicate her stomach. "And I can't think straight. Not with Becca and… I'm just so worried I can barely breathe. When I said I need to get back to Casper, I meant it. Something's wrong with my sister."

"Okay, it's okay." He'd wanted a different response, but she was worked up. "I understand. Take Connor and Lily home and help your sister. In a few days, you can come back and we can figure it out."

"You know I can't do that." Her eyebrows twisted as she frowned. "It's not that simple. I mean, Connor and Lily are a big part of my life. Ever since Grammy died, I've lived within a few miles of them. I'm like their second mom."

You know I can't do that. The words he wanted to say froze in his throat. He did know she couldn't. She'd been adamant about it from day one.

She shook her head, blowing out a breath and blinking at his chest. "Aaron left again, and what he said really hurt my sister. So I can't just drop the kids off with a 'see ya' when I know she's distraught. I can't do it. The worst thing is I don't even know if she'll be there."

He was confused. Sienna was leaving early and she didn't even know if her sister would be home? A twinge of anger stirred. "Then why are you going?"

"*Because* I don't know if she'll be there." She stared at him like, *don't you get it?* No, he didn't get it. Should he?

"Where would she be? How will you find her?" He took a small step to the side, raking his hand through his hair. "Why not stick around here until you know she's home?"

"You don't understand."

"You're right. I don't." It wouldn't be the first time, either. Why couldn't he be better at figuring out the things between the lines? He inched closer. The only words he still needed to say wouldn't be silenced. "I love you. I want to have a relationship with you. I can see us married, rocking on the backyard swing together for years to come. I want it all, and I know this is bad timing, but I don't see any other time we can have this discussion. I'm not trying to rush you. I just need you to know how I feel about you."

More tears sprouted from the corners of her eyes, and she covered her face with her hands. He groaned and pulled her into his arms, caressing her back, whispering *shh* in her hair.

He loved her. He wanted her here. And his heart was crumbling to dust because he didn't know how to convince her.

If he didn't convince her, she'd be gone. And his life would never be the same.

* * *

Sienna drew back, wishing she could stay wrapped in those strong arms forever. "I can't stay, Blaine. My family is in Casper. Your life is here. I wish it was different, but it isn't."

"I'm not asking you to give up your family. We have technology. You can FaceTime them every day. I'll drive you to Casper every weekend if you want."

She stared into his clear blue eyes and could see the honesty shining through. He really would drive her to Casper every weekend if she asked him to.

But she needed to be within walking distance of Becca and the kids. Just like she'd been for most of her life. Four hours away was too far if something went wrong.

Anger at Aaron shot through her. Why couldn't he have stayed and fought for his marriage? Then she wouldn't be so terrified of going back and finding no trace of her sister.

Did all men walk away when the going got tough?

"You *are* asking me to give them up." She rubbed her forearms, hardening her heart. "FaceTime doesn't cut it for me. I want to go to their school events. I like bringing them donuts on a random Friday morning. And there's the unexpected stuff, like what if Lily needs a ride home from band practice? Who will be there to pick her up?"

The way his jaw shifted warned her she was crossing lines she shouldn't.

"Her mother?" he said. "Her father?"

"Yeah, well, they haven't been all that reliable lately." Frustration mounted. He didn't get it. She was the one the kids relied on. She was the one they called.

"Okay, so a friend's parent could give her a ride. And Connor has his license. He could pick her up."

"That isn't the point."

"Then what is?"

"You're saying all the things that tempt me, Blaine. I enjoy working with your mother and Reagan and Holly. I've always loved Sunrise Bend. I like your friends. Like your church. Like this ranch. I like you. But everything you mentioned is on your terms."

"What do you mean?" His face scrunched in confusion.

"What would you be giving up?" she asked. "It never crossed your mind to leave your family behind. To leave this ranch and move down to Casper to be with me."

"What would I do there?" To his credit, he seemed curious, not mad. "All I know is ranching."

"I'm not asking you to move, Blaine. That's not what I'm getting at." Her shoulders fell. She felt tired. Drained.

"Then what are you getting at? Tell me what to do. Tell me what you want me to say." His voice rose in anguish, and she covered her ears, overcome by a sense of everything falling apart.

"First Troy, now this." She let out a strangled cry.

Blaine's arms were around her once more. His gaze probed her face. "What happened?"

"He called me earlier. He wants me to be the one to file the petition for him to waive his parental rights. And he thought I'd be gloating over his diagnosis. It's like he never knew me at all. Why would I ever be happy to learn someone I cared about has a serious illness? And I'm dumbfounded he expects me to be involved in this. Doesn't he get that I'm the one who loses either way? Just like now."

As soon as the speech left her mouth, she covered her lips, horrified by everything festering inside her.

Blaine's arms fell down to his sides. His silence crushed her.

She took a few jagged breaths until her heart rate slowed to normal.

"I love you, Sienna." His words flowed slowly and sweetly, like honey drizzling from a spoon.

"I love you, too, but it's not enough."

"Yes, it is. I love you."

"Then let me go." Her heart broke as she said what needed saying. "I can't give you what you need. What you deserve. I can't move here and live happily ever after."

He stared at her for a long moment, then asked, "Why not?"

"Because I'm the glue holding it together in Casper. I would be a nervous wreck here. Love doesn't conquer everything. My feelings for you won't change reality."

Blaine was offering her everything. But what good would it be if it meant leaving behind her precious loved ones?

She brushed past him to leave. She couldn't stay any longer. She needed to get the kids to pack their stuff. They'd hit the road as soon as they said goodbye to the rest of Blaine's family.

Everyone she cared about expected her to make these big, life-changing decisions.

She didn't have the energy to make them anymore. She just needed to get back to her ordinary life. Or what was left of it.

Chapter Thirteen

"If your parents agree you can have him, I'll drive Sushi to you in a few weeks." Blaine hugged Lily, then Connor, and cast a sideways glance at Sienna. They had said their goodbyes to everyone fifteen minutes ago and driven straight back to the cabin to load her vehicle. While Blaine and Connor stacked everything in the back of the SUV, Lily had gone back to his house to kiss the puppies goodbye. When she returned, she still had Sushi in her arms.

"Thank you so much. I know Mom and Dad will let us keep him," Lily said with tears in her eyes, hugging Sushi one last time. She kissed the puppy's forehead. "'Bye for now, sweet baby." She handed the pup back to Blaine. "Will you text me pictures of him?"

"I sure will." He adjusted the squirming dog in his arms, and the little guy calmed right down.

"Send pictures of Ollie, too, for me." Connor looked torn.

"I'll do that." He nodded to each of them. "Anytime you want to visit, the door's open."

"Alright, we'd better hit the road." Sienna held up her

keychain. Blaine sprang into action, opening the driver's side door for her. She got settled in her seat and looked up at him.

He didn't want to meet her gaze. Didn't want to see the rejection there.

Did she feel even the smallest fraction of what he felt for her? She'd said she loved him, but she couldn't mean it, not if she was leaving. He kept hoping she'd pull him aside and tell him she'd thought it over and decided to come back after returning the kids to her sister.

But his love wasn't enough for her. She didn't believe love conquered all.

Could have fooled him.

Before he did something stupid, like get on his knees and beg her to reconsider, he tapped his knuckles twice on the top of the vehicle.

"Take care now." He pulled down the tip of his cowboy hat to her and couldn't resist one last look at her pretty face. It was drawn, sad. Maybe she had regrets. He didn't know.

"You, too." Then she closed her door, held her hand up in goodbye and drove away.

As the vehicle grew smaller in the distance, so did his heart.

The timing had been wrong.

Maybe he should have opened up about his feelings sooner. Maybe he hadn't offered her what she really wanted. What *did* she really want?

He kicked at the gravel and took the puppy, now asleep, back to the house. Tried to clear his mind as he climbed the porch steps and let himself inside. After returning Sushi to Tiara and the other puppies, Blaine got a caged-in feeling and headed out to the pole barn.

Keep busy. Don't think about her.

He'd bury himself in what he knew. The ranch.

But as he pushed the button for the pole barn's overhead door to open, his mind was filled with their earlier conversation.

She'd accused him of wanting her on his terms. Of not giving anything up. And then she'd mentioned her ex—like Blaine could ever be compared to that guy.

A stack of boxes near the wall caught his attention. Spare parts for the tractors. He hefted one up and carried it to the back storage room, where he'd built shelves the previous winter. After shoving it on an empty shelf, he returned to move the other boxes.

She was wrong. He wasn't only thinking of himself. He was thinking of her, too. Sunrise Bend did have a lot to offer.

He frowned, wiping his forehead with the back of his hand. Maybe he *had* been selfish.

She liked her job in Casper. Her sister and the kids were her life. She felt responsible for them and wanted to be there. How could he fault her for that? He couldn't.

Memories of all the things she'd mentioned about her family trickled in. How her brother drowned and it had devastated all of them. Then her father left—more like disappeared—and no one was the same. And later her mom took off, too.

Sienna and Becca only had each other. Well, except for Aaron, who might well be out of the picture, too, at this point.

Maybe he hadn't fully understood her situation.

He hefted another box in his arms and carried it to the back room. If their places had been switched and Blaine knew Jet was struggling with something, wouldn't he drop everything to help his brother?

Bad comparison. Jet never struggled with anything he couldn't handle. Blaine wouldn't need to drop everything.

But Cody... Cody had been different.

In the back room, he set the heavy box on the floor, no longer caring if it made it onto a shelf.

What if it was Cody who needed him?

Regret shot through his torso. Blaine had always worried about the kid. He'd been a risk-taker. Bored. Easily lured into trouble. And even when Blaine and Jet told him to knock it off, he'd always fallen back into his bad habits. It had been so frustrating. And he'd been helpless to do anything about it.

That had been the worst part of Cody leaving and refusing to answer his calls and texts—he'd had no way of knowing if his brother was okay or not.

Sienna was in a similar position with her sister, and even more, she was like a second mom to those kids.

No wonder she'd left. No wonder she hadn't considered returning.

After being abandoned by her dad, her mom and even her ex-husband, she probably couldn't handle the idea of her sister being out of her life, too.

Shaken, he dropped his face into his hands. Where did that leave him?

He couldn't move to Casper. His skills involved raising cattle and growing hay, and that was about it. Plus, this ranch was his. He was a third-generation rancher, and he couldn't imagine walking away from it.

But could he imagine a future without Sienna?

Any future without her looked gray and miserable, as sparse and brittle as the dead pasture had been last year.

The clunk of footsteps had him straightening.

Jet was standing in the doorway. "I thought I'd find you back here."

"Oh, yeah?" He wiped his palms on his jeans and brushed past Jet on his way out of the room. "What do you need?"

"I don't need anything." Jet followed him to the open bay, filled with light.

"Then why are you here?" Blaine uncapped a dry-erase marker and pretended to read the list on the whiteboard.

"Just making sure you're okay."

"I'm fine." Blaine glanced over his shoulder at him. "Why wouldn't I be?"

"Oh, I don't know. Maybe because the woman you love just drove away."

He stilled. How did his brother know all that? Slowly, he turned to face him. A younger Blaine would have denied his love, but he didn't see the point now.

"What do you do?" He shrugged. "That's life for you."

Jet widened his eyes, trailing his finger down the side of the whiteboard. "That's your response? You're just going to let her go?"

"Yep." He eyed the other boxes, tempted to haul them to the back room to get away from his brother.

"Really?"

"What do you want me to say, Jet? Did you come over to gloat? I messed it up with Sienna, the same as I messed it up with the dead pasture and about a million other things over the years. Are you happy?"

"What are you talking about?" Jet looked genuinely

perplexed. "You didn't mess up the dead pasture. The drought did that. To be honest, I was surprised you got as much yield as you did out of it. You were smart to plant the wheatgrass."

Normally, his praise would have put a bounce in Blaine's step for days, but it didn't matter now. Nothing did.

"Yeah, well, I'd be shocked if I have enough hay to feed my cattle this winter." He bent to pick up another box and thought better of it. He might as well have the full conversation with Jet now. Then he could move on and get back to his life. His lonely, empty life.

"Does Sienna know you love her?" Jet asked quietly.

Blaine nodded.

"And she still left?"

He nodded again.

"Did you say something stupid?"

"Probably. I mean, I didn't think I did, but now I'm not so sure." Blaine headed toward the office and gestured for Jet to follow him. Inside, they both sprawled out on chairs.

"Why don't you run it by me?" Jet asked. "I won't judge. You know how much I messed up with Holly."

That brought a brief smile to Blaine's face.

"Sienna's close with her sister—Connor and Lily's mother. In fact, she's kind of a second mom to the kids. She's worried because Aaron—their father—took off. It had been looking like they'd resolved their marriage issues."

"Ouch." Jet leaned back. "So she left early for Becca's sake."

"Yeah."

"See? That's good."

"It's not good." Blaine ran his tongue across his teeth. "Her ex is hassling her. Doesn't want anything to do with the baby. Apparently, he called her today. I didn't know this before I asked her to stay."

"But you did ask her to stay?"

He nodded, his throat painfully tight.

"What else?"

Blaine gave him the short version of the conversation. "The worst thing about it is she's right. I'm asking her to give up everything, while I give up nothing."

"You're also offering a lot of things she doesn't have." Jet leaned forward. Neither spoke for a while. "Now what?"

"I don't know."

"If you love her and want to be with her, we'll figure out something with the ranch. We can join the two herds together again, or we can hire a manager. Maybe in time, she'll come around to living here."

"You'd be willing to do that? After all the trouble I gave you about splitting it up last year?"

"Of course, Blaine. You're not just my brother. You're my best friend. I want to see you happy."

The words healed the part of him that had felt like a runner-up to Jet most of his life. Reagan was right. They were different people. Blaine was who he was, and it was time to stop feeling like he didn't measure up.

"Thanks, Jet. You're my best friend, too."

"So go after her."

"That's the thing. I love Sienna, but I don't know if I could be happy in Casper. I only know ranching. And I don't want to leave it. It fulfills me, you know?"

"I do know." Jet stood. "You don't have to make any decisions tonight. Give it time. It will work out."

Blaine rose, too, and they made their way through the pole barn to the driveway, where Jet had parked.

"If you need me, I'm here." Jet pulled him in for a half hug. Blaine returned it.

"Thanks, man."

He stood there for a while after Jet drove away. Was his brother right? Would it work out?

He didn't know. Sienna hadn't exactly been overwhelmed by his declaration of love. And she'd flat-out refused to even consider pursuing a relationship with him.

The one thing he did know, however, was that she'd move mountains to help her sister, but she wouldn't consider staying a few extra hours to be with him.

He didn't want to be anyone's afterthought. He didn't want to be a distant second or third or fourth in her life.

He was done being the runner-up.

And that meant this fantasy of spending his life with Sienna had to end. He'd only be crushed if he held on to hope any longer.

After the first hour on the road, the urgency to make sure Becca was okay began to subside. And each mile of lonely highway brought new insights into her conversation with Blaine.

She was driving away from the most incredible man she'd ever met. A life with him would mean a life of happiness. The love she'd never dreamed possible waited for her in Sunrise Bend, and she'd turned him down.

Leaving her family and life in Casper was too big a risk.

Connor hadn't said much on the ride so far. He'd been staring out the passenger window. And Lily had been quiet in the back seat, too. Neither of them had put up a fight when she'd told them they needed to leave early, which had surprised her. Sienna felt bad for ending their time on the ranch prematurely, even if it was only by a day.

In time, they'd all get back into their routines. She'd get the nursery ready and start putting a game plan together for after the baby was born. School would start back up at the end of August. The kids would talk Becca into keeping Sushi, Sienna had no doubt. They'd have the puppy to keep them busy, and she'd have the baby.

"Aunt Sienna?" Lily asked from the back seat.

"Yes?" She smiled at her in the rearview mirror.

"I went to Blaine's earlier to check on the puppies."

"I'm sure he appreciated it."

She kept her eyes downcast. "I knocked, but no one came, and then I heard voices, so I let myself in."

A fearful sensation set her nerves on edge. "Oh?"

"I stopped in the hall when I heard you and Blaine talking. I didn't mean to eavesdrop, but…"

Sienna gripped the steering wheel, wondering how much her niece had heard.

"I told Conner, and we think you should be with Blaine. He's the greatest guy, Aunt Sienna." Her hazel eyes brightened. "We know you love Sunrise Bend. Everyone's so nice, and you love making the candles."

Sienna glanced at Connor. He'd shifted to face her fully.

"Lil's right. The ranch is awesome, and Blaine's a good guy. He'd make you happy."

She swallowed the emotions their words evoked. "You two make me happy. Your mom makes me happy."

Connor looked back at Lily.

"We're getting older," Lily said. "We can deal with Mom. If she gets sad, we'll hug her and be there for her."

"And you're always telling me it's not my job to worry about her problems," Connor said. "I can set limits and still love her. She has the counselor now. She can call him if she's upset."

So Connor *had* been listening to her all these months.

"She can always call me, too." Sienna gave him a tender smile. "It won't be easy, you know. Sometimes it's hard setting limits when it's your mom."

"I know." He shrugged. "The thing is, though, no matter how long I listen to her talk about Dad or listen to her cry, it's never enough. I used to think it helped her when I listened. But now I'm not so sure. Nothing really changes, you know? It's the same thing the next night."

His words were a jolt of truth to her heart.

Nothing did really change. Being there unconditionally for her sister never made much of a difference. No matter how much she sacrificed to be there for Becca, it wasn't enough.

Is that how I feel? Like I'm sacrificing for her?

She'd always told herself she was there for Becca because she loved her. But right now—driving back early—it didn't feel like love. It felt like fear. She was scared Becca would fall apart without her. But her sister had been falling apart for months.

Becca was a wonderful sister, a good mom. She was just going through a rough patch.

"We think you should go back to Blaine after you take us home," Lily said. "We know you like him. You're all smiley and holding hands all the time. He's perfect for you."

He was perfect for her.

But she wasn't perfect for him.

Sienna had left the one person who accepted her, asked nothing from her except for her presence.

He simply wanted to be with her, liked being near her.

He was the one man who loved her unconditionally.

Yeah, for now.

If Sienna took a chance and moved to Sunrise Bend, she had no guarantees Blaine wouldn't wake up one day and realize he'd made a mistake, that he didn't want to be with her. Just like her parents had. Just like Troy had.

No matter what Connor and Lily said, they needed her around. Becca did, too. And she wasn't about to let them go. Even if it meant losing the man who'd captured her heart.

Blaine stood in front of his bedroom window late that night watching the stars in the black sky. Even in the darkness, he could make out Grandpa's swing. He turned away. All he could see was Sienna's smiling face as she sat there with him night after night.

And now she was gone.

He padded down the hall and peeked in on the puppies. He'd brought Ollie in to sleep with Tiara and the pups, and they'd all curled up together, sleeping peacefully. Together at last.

He doubted he'd get any shut-eye tonight. Continuing to the kitchen, he wrestled with his thoughts. Anger began to build.

God, why did You bring her here, just to take her away? Why did You even let me get close to her? It would have been better if she had stayed a distant memory. Then I wouldn't be going through this.

He entered the kitchen and whipped open the fridge.

Bending to scan the contents, he shook his head and slammed the door shut. He wasn't hungry. Wasn't thirsty.

He was mad.

Mad at himself for bungling the conversation with her earlier.

Mad at her for not responding the way he wanted.

Mad at Jet for even suggesting he leave the ranch.

Mad at God for allowing this to happen.

Blaine pivoted and stalked over to the couch. He sat, then leaned his head back on the cushion so he could stare at the ceiling.

Did he matter at all to Sienna? Had she given him the slightest thought since driving away?

He'd been tempted to call her tonight when he knew she would be back in Casper. He'd wanted to find out if her sister was okay and to hear her voice.

But he'd decided against it. He'd said his part. She'd said hers. End of story.

Wiping his hands down his cheeks, he shook his head. He didn't matter to her. Not the way she mattered to him.

He must not have mattered much to Cody, either. Had his brother even looked at the handful of texts he'd sent? Listened to the voice mail he'd left?

Did Blaine really matter to anyone in the grand scheme of things?

Jet was right. The ranches could be rejoined. A manager could be hired. If Blaine decided to move a million miles away, his family would wish him well and their lives would go on as usual.

No one needed him.

Like a popped water balloon, all the anger he'd been holding spilled out. He sat there clenching and unclenching his fists. He'd always taken life as it came. Hadn't questioned much. Knew his place. Knew what to do in most circumstances.

But right here, right now, felt like a crossroads. And he recognized he had a choice.

Bitterness or acceptance.

God, forgive me. I'm like an angry bull knocking my horns against a fence to tear it down. You've answered so many of my prayers over the years. I just wanted You to answer this one, too. I love her. I love that redhead. She's smart and calm and fun. Easy to be with. I've never felt so full of life as when I'm with her.

He let all the good memories wash over him. Soon the anger, the bitterness shifted to something more painful. To loss. To regret.

Lord, I want it my way. I don't like giving her up. But I have to. I know it worked out with Jet and Holly, but I'm not my brother. Never have been. And Sienna left because her family is more important to her than me.

Was he wrong? Maybe she was scared of losing them.

He knew that fear well.

It was time to be completely honest with himself about Cody. He'd been clinging to his final memories of his brother—bad memories—but in the months after he left the ranch, Cody had gotten his life together. Holly had said so. She also believed he would have reconciled with them all eventually. According to Holly, Cody had been happy.

So why was he still holding on to this guilt?

Sienna had told him to let it go, that he'd been forgiven. The scripture the pastor had spoken about earlier this summer came back.

Remember ye not the former things, neither consider the things of old. Behold, I will do a new thing—now it shall spring forth, shall ye not know it? I will even make a way in the wilderness, and rivers in the desert.

He was ready to make peace with Cody's death. God was in the business of making ways in the wilderness and rivers in the desert.

God, I convinced myself I was to blame for Cody's problems. But I wasn't. We all have free will. Sienna does. Her sister does, too, although Sienna might not like it. Would You get through to her? Help her see she isn't responsible for her sister's, Connor's or Lily's happiness?

Blaine clasped his hands behind his head. Better times with Cody trickled back to him, ones he'd forgotten. Of riding around the ranch on horseback, of stopping at the candy store in town after church on Sunday, of Christmas mornings and all kinds of things he hadn't thought about in years.

He wasn't sure what he was going to do about Sienna, but he knew one thing. Jet was right. Time would work this out. And he'd be okay.

Sienna knocked again on their front door as Connor fumbled to find his key. A sense of dread brewed in her gut. They hadn't stopped along the way, and the night sky held an ominous breeze.

Was her sister home? Or had she taken off? Like Dad? Like Mom?

Please, God, don't do that to Connor and Lily. Please let her be home.

"Got it." Connor held up the key with a lopsided grin and moved to insert it in the lock at the exact moment the door opened.

Becca was standing in the foyer, looking surprised,

and Aaron was next to her with his arm around her shoulders.

"What are you doing back? I thought you were coming home tomorrow." Becca opened her arms wide to hug the kids, and they moved inside, hugging both parents as Sienna squeezed into the foyer and shut the door behind her.

"When you called earlier, I was worried." Sienna couldn't keep the edge out of her tone. She'd packed everything in a hurry, said their goodbyes in a rush and practically peeled out of Blaine's life to get here. And what did she find? Becca had been here with Aaron all along?

"I texted you more than once." Sienna took out her phone and pointed to it. "Didn't you get my messages?"

"Oh, no. Sorry." Becca flushed, looking up at Aaron. "We, ah, had a long talk."

He squeezed her shoulders. "I'm back. For good. And I can't wait to make up for lost time."

"Mom—Mom, guess what?" Lily clasped her hands near her chest and started bouncing up and down. "Blaine is letting us keep one of the puppies. Sushi! He was the runt of the litter, the one I told you about. I took care of him every day. He's bringing him here in two weeks!"

"A puppy?" Becca shot Sienna a questioning glance. "I don't know about that."

Aaron had pulled Connor into a hug. "I think a puppy is a great idea, Bec."

"You do?" Her face lit up. "Well, if you two promise to take care of him, feed him, fill his water bowl, walk him, then I guess we'll take him. He's your responsibility, though."

"We will!" Connor and Lily said in unison. They met each other's eyes and laughed.

"Come on, you can tell me all about your summer while we unload your stuff." Aaron opened the door, and they turned and went outside, leaving her alone with Becca.

The happy family reunion was everything Sienna wanted for the kids and her sister, but she couldn't help feeling betrayed. She motioned for Becca to join her in the kitchen.

"After your call, I couldn't help but think the worst." Sienna leaned against the counter. "I didn't know what I was going to find when I got here. I didn't even know if you'd be here."

"Where would I go?" Becca frowned.

"I don't know. But it wouldn't be the first time I walked into an empty house."

"I'm not Dad. I'm not Mom." Her chin rose. "That's what you're getting at, right?"

"I didn't say you were." But, yeah, she was getting at that.

"Look, Sienna, I know I've got issues, but abandoning my family isn't one of them. I really don't appreciate you implying I would do that."

The need to defend herself rose up.

"Aaron and I made some decisions today," Becca said. "We're continuing to go to counseling until the counselor thinks it's no longer necessary. And I'm going to see someone else—a therapist—to work through things regarding Dan and our parents."

Sienna clamped her mouth shut, frowning. All of that sounded good, but she couldn't let go of the anger pressing inside her.

Becca reached over and placed her hand on Sienna's shoulder. "You might want to see a professional about Dan and our parents, too."

"Me?" Why would Becca think she needed therapy?

"We dealt with our childhood traumas in different ways." Her sad smile was full of love. "I know I've been too clingy and emotional. And maybe you've had to step into the role of being a parent too many times." Becca held up her hands, palms out in defense. "That's on me. I'm going to work on it."

Sienna kept her spine rigid as the words spun circles around her mind. The anger subsided as she recognized the truth in her sister's words.

"I think you're right, Becca." In some ways it was a relief to hear her sister's honesty. But she also felt duped. Like she'd gotten sucked into her sister's drama for so long…and it hadn't been necessary.

She'd been blaming Becca for her need to live in Casper, to stay close to the kids, but was it even true?

"I'm glad you and Aaron are working things out." She choked down the sadness. "But I'm not going to pretend I'm not upset we left the ranch early for nothing. You should have called me."

Connor and Lily entered the room, cheerfully chatting with their father. Sienna had to face facts. The kids were right—they were getting older. And from the looks of it, their family would work through any issues that came up.

But where did that leave her?

Alone. They didn't need her. They all had each other.

Too hurt to stay any longer, Sienna turned to go.

"Wait, Sienna." Becca sighed. "I didn't mean to upset you. I haven't even thanked you for everything. For taking the kids this summer. For giving Aaron and I the space to work on our marriage. I couldn't have done this without you. How can I ever repay you?"

Becca hugged her tightly, and some of the tension eased.

"We're sisters. That's what we're here for." Sienna attempted to smile. It was true, too. They'd always had each other's backs. "I'm going to take off. I'm pretty tired."

"Are you sure?" she asked. "Why don't you stay a while?"

Sienna shook her head. "I don't think so."

After hugging everyone goodbye, Sienna drove the short distance to her apartment, rolled her suitcase to the entrance, unlocked the front door and went inside. It smelled stale. She flicked the lights on. A standard two-bedroom, it was clean, beige and tidy. It felt sterile. Lonely.

She kicked off her shoes. Leaving the suitcase in the living room, she padded straight to the bedroom, pulled back the covers and climbed into her bed. Only then did the tears begin to fall.

She'd left Blaine and Sunrise Bend and the candle shop and her friends behind. She'd left them to make sure Becca was okay.

And Becca was okay.

Better than okay.

It was what she'd wanted. But now she was questioning everything.

Her sister had been through life crises more than once, and she'd never walked out on the kids. She'd never vanished like their mom and dad had. Becca was a lot of things—emotional, prone to anxiety, even self-centered at times—but she wasn't like their parents.

Had Sienna been projecting her fears of being abandoned on her sister?

She burrowed deeper into the covers.

Blaine's face—his handsome, hurt, devastated face—had etched itself into her mind. He'd told her he loved her. Given her an alternative to her life here. And what had she done?

She'd accused him of not giving anything up. And it wasn't even the reason she'd left.

Sienna had trust issues that would fill a quarry. She hadn't trusted her sister to do right by Connor and Lily. She hadn't trusted Aaron to stick around for his family. She hadn't even trusted Connor and Lily to be able to handle their parents' problems.

But most of all she hadn't trusted herself.

Lord, what's wrong with me? I never really loved Troy. That's why when he left me, I didn't fall apart like Becca did. Blaine's everything I want. And I'm scared. I'm so scared. Help me!

Sitting up, she grabbed the Bible from her nightstand. With the flip of the switch, the lamp glowed, and she turned to the back of the Bible for the subject index. Trailing her finger down, she stopped on the section marked Trust.

She paged through and found the first five passages, but they weren't what she was looking for. The sixth one, though, watered her parched soul.

O taste and see that the Lord is good: blessed is the man that trusteth in him.

The Lord was good. She closed the Bible. She had only to look at what happened this evening to taste and see His goodness.

Becca and Aaron had reunited. They still had a bumpy

journey ahead, but they were committed to each other. If God could work on Becca's heart to take the scary leap of seeing a therapist and continuing to go to couples' counseling with Aaron, surely God could help Sienna trust that He had good things in store for her as well.

Lord, please forgive me for thinking the worst earlier about my sister. I didn't realize how much my parents' actions affected me. I didn't realize how much I haven't trusted anyone to stick around.

The pain and emotional turmoil of the past day eased. Her eyelids drooped as exhaustion overtook her. She needed to make things right with Blaine. She just didn't know how.

Chapter Fourteen

Blaine woke the next morning with a throbbing headache. The puppies were whining in the spare room. He swung his legs over the side of the bed, wiped his hands down his cheeks and let out a loud sigh. The three hours of sleep had not helped him. Sienna was still gone.

He made his way down the hall to the spare room, then petted Tiara and Ollie, filled their water bowls and allowed the two adult dogs out of the room. They trotted straight to the sliding door leading to the backyard. After he let them out, he stared at the beautiful landscape with low hills in the distance and cattle moving out of his view. Pastel pinks and purples colored the sky. The sun was waking up, and he had decisions to make.

Blaine would be willing to give up the ranch and move to Casper, but not under these circumstances. Sienna had made it clear her family came first. If he moved to be near her, he would be accepting the position of being the runner-up in her life.

He wasn't willing to stay in the shadows when it came to love. His friends had shown him the importance of mutual love and respect.

But just because Sienna couldn't put him first now didn't mean she couldn't later. And if her feelings did change—if she could love him wholeheartedly to the point he wasn't second-best—well, then he might be willing to move to Casper to be with her.

It would be hard. But it would be worth it.

The dogs chased each other outside for a few minutes. Then they stopped several feet apart. Ollie's ears perked as he let out two barks. Tiara bent her front legs, then took off with Ollie chasing her. They finally slowed, sniffing each other affectionately before playing again.

It looked like they were in no hurry to come back inside, so he retreated to the kitchen and prepped the coffeemaker. Once it was filled, he pressed the on button and returned to his spot in front of the sliding door. The dogs were panting as they lay near each other on the lawn. They looked like they didn't have a care in the world.

That's how it was with Sienna. When he was with her, it felt like they were in sync. Like he didn't have a care in the world. Until yesterday.

As the coffeemaker sputtered, he thought about his options.

He could give Sienna space.

He could call her to see how she was doing.

Or could he try to forget about her and move on with his life.

No. He couldn't forget her. She was impossible to forget.

He had another option. He could do things the old-fashioned way. He could court her.

Staring unseeing out toward the hills, he mulled over the concept. It might work. He could go down there on weekends…for as long as it took. Maybe it would prove to her he'd never abandon her.

The way they'd left things felt jagged and raw. What if he drove down there today? He'd tell her what was on his mind. Assure her he'd be at her apartment every Saturday to prove not all men walked away when the going got tough.

It was the only idea that made sense at this point.

The coffeemaker beeped as the dogs trotted toward the sliding door. Blaine let them in, petting both before pouring himself a cup of coffee.

He and Sienna could make their relationship work. He was sure of it. Sienna just didn't know it yet.

Sienna woke to the sound of cartoons blasting through the paper-thin walls. One eye struggled to open. Then the other. Her body felt as heavy as solid iron. The baby's arms and legs rolled around in her tummy, and she groaned, smiling.

"I see you're awake, too. It won't be long before you'll be begging to watch cartoons like the neighbors." She hauled herself out of bed and made the mistake of glancing at the mirror. Splotchy face. Hair a disaster. Shaking her head, she forced herself to look away.

After showering, she debated whether she should unpack her car first or head to a drive-through for breakfast. Either way she had to figure out what to do about Blaine soon.

She couldn't leave things the way they were now.

The man likely had no idea how deep her feelings were for him. And she hated that she'd given him the impression he wasn't important to her.

He was important. Very important.

Someone knocked on the door. She went to the entrance, figuring it was Becca, and looked through the peephole.

Erica? What was she doing here?

Sienna unlocked the door and ushered her inside. Erica held two iced coffees and a white bag Sienna recognized from her favorite coffee shop.

"Mom told me you came back early, and I thought I'd surprise you." Erica set the coffees and bag on the nearby table and gave Sienna a warm hug. "How are you?"

"Better now that you're here." She smiled and pointed to the coffees. "Which one is mine?"

"They're both decaf iced mochas. Oh, and I brought donuts. I figured half a dozen should get us through catching up. And, boy, do we have some catching up to do."

As Sienna took her iced coffee along with a glazed donut to the couch, she was grateful for Erica's friendship. They'd gotten each other through some difficult times all year, and it was time for her to be honest with her friend.

As soon as Erica had settled into the comfy chair kitty-corner to her, Sienna took a deep breath. "I'm in love with Blaine."

Closing her eyes, she waited for laughter or condemnation, but when neither came, she opened them one at a time. Erica simply took another bite of a chocolate cake donut and nodded.

"You're perfect for him. And he's perfect for you."

"I'm sorry I didn't tell you earlier."

She waved her off. "Don't be. I know it's complicated. You're dealing with Troy and the baby and your sister, not to mention working for my mom, who probably would drop to her knees in tears of joy at the thought of you and Blaine getting married. No—no need to apologize."

She fought back tears. Erica got her in a way few people did.

"And listen, I'm all for it. Blaine will never—and I mean never—let you down." Erica set the rest of her donut on a napkin as a pained expression crossed her face.

"What is it?" Sienna asked. "What's wrong? Is it the baby?"

"No." A wisp of a smile crossed her lips as she massaged her belly. "I was just thinking about Blaine and how I wish Jamie was a little more like him."

She didn't know what to say. Erica's husband had been on the road more and more, checking on their businesses. And he tended to get distracted easily—the few times she'd met him, he'd been more interested in looking at his phone than enjoying a dinner out.

"Does Blaine know?" Erica asked, tilting her head. "He's not the best at picking up on things."

Tears threatened as she thought of yesterday. She willed them away, holding her breath until she was reasonably sure she could talk without breaking down.

"I don't think he knows how much I care about him."

"That's probably for the best. I don't know if you could convince him to get serious with you, anyhow. He's not getting married. He's said it so many times, I couldn't begin to count. Oh, I'm sorry, that sounds harsh. I didn't mean to—"

"No, no, it's fine." Sienna let out a soft laugh. "Actually, he was the one who told me he loved me. Yesterday.

He wants me to move there, work at the candle shop. And date."

"And date?" Erica tried on the concept and seemed to like it, judging by her eager nod. "You know what this means, don't you?"

She shook her head.

"You've cracked the shell around the nut that is my stubborn, wonderful brother. Where all of us have tried, you're the only one to succeed. He must really be into you."

She could feel the heat rising to her cheeks. "Well, I'm pretty into him."

"Yet, here you are."

"Yeah, yesterday was pretty bad." She told Erica about getting Becca's call and how worried she'd been. Then they discussed Troy's phone call. And finally, Sienna gave her the briefest of recaps on how she and Blaine had left things. "I don't know what to do. I love him, and I hurt him, and I don't think he'll ever believe I could put him first at this point. I said a lot of things I'm not sure I even believe anymore."

Erica made a production out of wiping the crumbs off her hands. Then she gripped the sides of the chair and stood up.

"You're going to tell him. Everything. He can take it. If anyone in my family can take the whole truth, it's Blaine. In fact, he needs it from you. Tell him everything you just told me."

"What if he doesn't believe me?"

"Give him time."

"What if I'm not ready? I mean, I've been here for my sister and the kids for so long, I'd feel like I'm abandoning them."

Erica closed the distance between them and took her hands in hers. Sienna rose to stand, still holding her hands.

"Whatever happens with Becca and Aaron and the kids, you'll be there for them. You will always be there for them. Whether you're in Sunrise Bend or here in Casper. Don't worry about that. You love them. Blaine will understand as long as he knows he's first in your life."

Sienna pressed her lips together to keep her emotions under wraps and nodded. "I know you're right, but I worry…what if I can't put him first? What if I mess up and run off to Becca again when he needs me?"

"No one is perfect. Just do your best. Trust me, he will mess up, too. And you'll forgive him."

The biggest worry of all still lingered way back in the deepest recesses of her heart. She'd never allowed it to take form, but it was there. Had been there for most of her life.

"What if something happens and I shut down like my parents did?" she whispered. "What if I walk away from him and all we have? It's better to leave things the way they are now. I couldn't bear to think of him in that kind of pain."

Erica hugged her again. "Oh, Sienna, is that why you're worried?" She backed up, keeping her hands on Sienna's shoulders, and looked into her eyes. "You don't have it in you. You're strong when everyone around you crumbles. You take the waves head-on instead of sprinting in the other direction. You don't have to ever worry about walking away. You couldn't if you tried."

The tears came then, and she let Erica hold her as she cried for the little girl who'd lost her brother and her father all in the same year. And she cried for the teenager whose life had been upended when her mom walked away. She cried for her time in Sunrise Bend being cut short in high school. And she cried for the adult woman who'd married a man she didn't love because she hadn't been able to trust the real thing.

When all her tears had been shed, she excused herself and washed her face before returning to the living room.

"What are you going to do now?" Erica asked.

"I think I need to go back. Talk to Blaine face-to-face." She hadn't allowed herself to seriously consider what he'd offered. Until now. And she wanted it. Oh, how she wanted it!

"Good plan. Are you thinking today?"

"Yes. I need to do it before I lose my nerve." Would he welcome her, though? Or had she hurt him so badly he wanted nothing to do with her? "Should I call him and let him know?"

Erica grimaced. "He's probably out looking at cows."

"True. Plus, he might tell me not to bother."

They sat in silence. Then a knock on the door made them both jump. Sienna placed her hand over her heart. "Oh, that scared me. I'll be right back."

She went to the door and didn't bother checking the peephole this time. When she opened it, her jaw dropped to the floor.

Blaine!

She soaked him in, from his cowboy hat and shimmering blue eyes to his T-shirt, jeans and cowboy boots. He held a huge bouquet of red roses. She practically swooned.

He stepped forward, wrapping his arm around her waist. "Whoa, there. Are you okay?"

"Wonderful," she said breathlessly as she smiled up at him.

"Ahem."

They both looked toward the living room, where Erica was standing with both hands on her hips. Her big grin lightened the mood.

"Blaine, you are now officially the smartest brother in our family." She sailed over to him, bopped the brim of his cowboy hat and winked at Sienna. "I trust you two will figure things out."

Then she left, and the door clicked shut behind her.

"You're here." Sienna's pulse was racing faster than a rabbit being chased by a dog. "I was trying to figure out when and how to go back to the ranch. I never should have left like that."

He led her to the couch, where they both took a seat, shifting to face each other.

"I couldn't leave things the way we did." He took off his hat and set it on the end table. "I pushed you, I rushed you. Don't get me wrong, I meant everything I said, but you were right when you told me I wouldn't be giving anything up, and you would. I never really thought about how much you'd be giving up."

She pressed her hand to his cheek. "That's where you're wrong, Blaine. I'd been so focused on Becca and the kids that I didn't think about what I wanted. What I needed."

"What do you want? What do you need?"

You, Blaine. Only you.

Blaine prepared his heart for pain. Yesterday, he'd been somewhat certain she loved him and would want to stay and have a life with him. But now? He had no clue.

"When I got to Becca's house last night, Aaron was

there with her. And she acted surprised I would even think to return early."

"I guess that means they're okay?"

She nodded. "I think so. I mean, they're both taking the necessary steps to make their marriage work. But that's not my point."

He looked into her pleading green eyes and hoped she wasn't going to let him down again. Not when he'd gotten this far.

"I realized I was wrong to leave the way I did. I was afraid I'd get there and she'd be gone. I couldn't stand thinking of Connor and Lily going through what I'd been through with my parents. But I'd forgotten that Becca had been through the same thing. And I underestimated her. I underestimated them all."

He clenched his hands, thinking about how her childhood had affected her. No wonder she wanted to be close to her sister and the kids.

"Erica helped me see things more clearly."

When Erica was involved, he got nervous. She saw too much and said exactly what was on her mind.

"I've been afraid of losing the people I love." She ducked her chin, then met his gaze. "I couldn't deal with what you said yesterday because it scared me. And I didn't tell you all the things you need to know because I didn't believe they were possible for me."

Hope rose in his chest.

"I love you, Blaine. And last night when I walked into this empty apartment, I realized I'd made the wrong choice. I chose to cling to my sister and the kids, but they don't need me to hover around them. They want me to be happy, too."

He couldn't think of a thing to say. He waited for her to continue.

"The only time I've been truly happy is when I'm with you. I feel bad, Blaine, because I take from you more than I give. I needed you all summer. You were the one who made sure the kids had fun. You were the one who accepted me—divorced, pregnant and all. I don't deserve you, Blaine Mayer, but I sure do love you."

He crushed her in his arms, then whispered in her hair, "I love you, too. Oh, I love you."

Then he eased back and stared into her eyes, tucking her hair behind her ear.

"You have it all wrong, Sienna. You think of others before yourself. You put your life on hold for two months because you knew your family needed it. Connor and Lily needed the ranch, and their parents needed the time and space to work things out. And, frankly, when I think of how accommodating you've been with your ex, well, I'm humbled."

She smiled. "You think I should support him waiving his rights, don't you?"

"I think you know what's right for you and the baby. I admire the fact you're worried he'll regret it, even knowing having him around will only complicate things more. I will support you no matter what you decide. But I'm getting ahead of myself."

"What do you mean?" Her eyebrows drew together as she tilted her head.

"Look, I know you're having a baby—" he gave a pointed look at her bulging bump "—and asking you to move so far away from your sister this close to the baby coming was dumb of me. I want to be together, but I'm fine doing it on your terms. I'll drive down here on weekends and we can date. And if in time you think you'd be willing to move up by me, I'll pack your apartment myself if need be. But if you decide here is where you need to stay, I'm willing to move."

Her stunned expression made him pause.

"You okay?"

She nodded.

"But I've got to be honest, and I expect you to be honest right back." He shifted his jaw and hoped for the answer he wanted to hear. "I won't be second-best, Sienna. I will never ask you to give up your family, but I need to be first in your life if we're going to have a real go at this. I want it all—love, commitment. I've been around good marriages. My parents, my brother, my friends are all committed to their spouses. And I know I'm jumping the gun talking marriage, but for us to have something real, I need to know we're on the same page."

"We're on the same page." She nodded, smiling through shining eyes. "I'm sorry I made you feel that way, Blaine. I was wrong, and I know it. So, yes, you will be number one in my life. And I know now that you wouldn't ask me to ignore my family. There will be times Becca calls crying, and I will be taking those calls. And if Lily or Connor have an emergency, I'll be there for them. But you will always be first in my life."

"Does this mean we're going to try dating?" He couldn't stop staring at her lips. "I'll come every week."

"No, I don't think so."

His heart fell. Had he been reading her all wrong?

"My heart's always been in Sunrise Bend. It's time for me to be there permanently."

He needed to make sure he understood. "Okay, forgive me for being slow, but does this mean we'll be dating?"

She leaned forward, wrapping her arms around his neck, pressing her forehead to his.

"Oh, we're way past dating, Blaine Mayer."

The only reply he could think of was to claim her lips with his. And as he kissed her, he knew how blessed he was.

Sienna was his, and he couldn't wait to bring her home.

Chapter Fifteen

Two weeks later Sienna gave the counter a final wipe, then placed her hand on her aching lower back. Becca, Aaron and the kids would be here any minute to pick up Sushi, and she couldn't wait to see them. She walked onto the cabin's front porch, smiling at the blue sky. Blaine had stopped by twenty minutes ago, giving her a kiss before jogging down the lane to his house to shower off the smell of cattle before they arrived. How she loved that man.

The day Blaine had shown up at her apartment was still etched in her brain. After working things out, they'd called Erica to come back over and celebrated by going out to lunch. Then Sienna had taken him to Becca's house and introduced him to her and Aaron. The kids had been thrilled to see him.

The next day Blaine had helped her pack up the essentials of her apartment, and they'd driven separately back to the ranch. When she'd pulled up to the cabin, her heart had practically leaped for joy.

She was home.

And last weekend, they'd celebrated at Randy and Hannah's wedding with all of Blaine's friends.

"Hey, there, beautiful!" Blaine yelled, sauntering her way. If her belly wasn't so ginormous, she'd run to him and jump in his arms. But she'd have to be content waddling his way. He caught up to her and instantly pulled her close. The baby chose that moment to kick, and he grinned before kissing her.

"Hoo." She fanned herself when they broke away.

"Looks like you've got a feisty one in there." Keeping his arm around her waist, he led her back to the porch. "Sit down. Rest."

She smiled. She heard those words ten times a day from him, Julie, Reagan, Holly—and even little Clara had told her to "west" this week. They'd all welcomed her back, and Julie had shed a few tears of joy. Sienna would always treasure the moment.

A vehicle approached.

"They're here." Blaine stood wide-legged on the top step of the porch, staring at the drive. "Lily's going to be disappointed the other puppies all went to their homes already."

"Any disappointment will vanish as soon as Sushi is back in her arms."

"True."

The SUV stopped in front of the cabin, and her family poured out. Aaron went straight to Blaine, shaking his hand, while Becca held her arms out as she climbed the steps to Sienna. They hugged for a long time.

"Looks like this one's coming soon, huh, sis?" Becca stared at her baby bump.

"Any minute." She rubbed her belly. "I'm not sure how I feel about it."

"You're going to be a great mom. Are you sure you don't want me to be your birthing partner?"

"It's too far. I'll be okay. Julie was ecstatic when I asked her. She's been through it five times."

Becca pressed the side of her head to Sienna's. A surge of love for her sister made her smile. Becca had been seeing the therapist, and Sienna had been talking to Blaine's pastor about her own issues from the past. Their relationship felt safer than it had in a long time.

"Aunt Sienna!" Lily hugged her, barely getting her arms around the baby bump. "I miss you."

"I miss you, too." She gently caressed Lily's hair. "I'm glad you're here now."

"Me, too. I can't wait to bring Sushi home."

"Hey, Connor, I see your best friend found you." She nodded to Ollie, who'd raced over as soon as they'd gotten out of the vehicle.

"I missed this guy." Connor laughed, scratching behind both of Ollie's ears.

"Come on in." Sienna gave Becca and Aaron the tour of the cabin, and then they all went over to Blaine's, where Tiara and Sushi were sitting in the hallway waiting.

"Oh, there you are!" Lily ran to Sushi and dropped to her knees. She took the pup in her arms and hugged him, kissing the top of his furry head. "You're coming home with us today."

Blaine crouched beside her. "I'm glad this guy's going to the best home. Remember how you worried he wouldn't make it those first days?"

She nodded, her eyes glistening. Then she shifted to put her arms around Blaine's neck and gave him a quick hug.

"Thank you, Blaine. This was the best summer of my life."

Becca and Aaron reached for each other's hands, exchanging a loving look.

"Yes, we want to thank you, too," Becca said to Blaine as he rose. His face was flaming. "Thank you for all you did for these two this summer."

He nodded, and Sienna moved to his side. He put his arm around her shoulders.

"Maybe Connor and Lily could come next summer, too," Sienna said.

Blaine shot her a quick glance. Then a smile spread across his face. "Why didn't I think of that?"

"Do you mean it?" Connor asked, his eyes full of hope.

"Yes." Blaine nodded. "Absolutely."

"Can Tiara have puppies again when I come?" Lily asked, holding Sushi, who was licking her chin.

"I hope so." Blaine chuckled. "I'll need your help."

Sienna leaned her head against his shoulder. She couldn't have imagined in June that she'd be living in Sunrise Bend full-time and hosting her happily married sister, her brother-in-law and the kids for the day. Oh, and inviting them to spend the summer with her next year.

Here, with Blaine and his family, anything felt possible. Just as it had in high school.

She'd found her home in Sunrise Bend. And she couldn't wait to see what was in store next.

One week later, Blaine paced the hospital hall. What was taking so long? Surely, she should have had the baby by now?

His mom came out of Sienna's room. "Blaine, honey, Sienna's asking for you. It's a girl!"

He raced into the room to see Sienna's radiant face as she held her precious bundle wrapped in a blanket near her chest. Blaine moved to stand next to her, staring in awe at the tiny baby.

"Look at her little fingernails, Blaine." Sienna stared up at him then, and he got choked up.

"She's beautiful. Just like her mother." He grazed the baby's hand with a feather-light touch. "What are you going to name her?"

"Madeline." She smiled. "I always liked that name."

"Well, Madeline, welcome to the world."

He gave Sienna the softest kiss on the lips he could manage, and they stared, smiling, at the baby for what felt like hours.

When the nurse came to move her and the baby to another room, Blaine assured Sienna he'd meet her there as soon as he let the family know the room number.

With a sense of awe and pride, he strode down the hall to where his family was waiting. His dad gave him a hug, then Jet and Holly congratulated him, and Reagan carried Clara over. He took his adorable niece in his arms. "Are you ready to meet your cousin?"

"Yay!" She clapped her little hands.

"Let's hope she's ready for a brother or sister, too," Holly murmured.

"What?" his mom yelled. She must have supersonic hearing—he was convinced of it. "Are you…? Is this…? Are you…?"

"Mom, we're having a baby." Jet gave Mom a deadpan stare. "We found out a few hours ago."

"Oh, praise Jesus!"

Blaine pulled Jet into a hug. "Congratulations, man."

"You, too, brother." Jet clapped his hand on his shoulder. "You're going to make a great daddy…when you finally propose. Don't you think it's time?"

"Soon." Blaine grinned. As usual, Jet was right, and this time it didn't bother him at all.

Just then Becca, Aaron, Connor and Lily rushed into the lobby. "We got here as soon as we could. Are we too late?"

"It's a girl," Blaine announced. "Mama and daughter are fine."

And he'd make sure they were fine for the rest of their lives. He couldn't wait to make Sienna and Madeline his. To cherish and protect them forever.

Epilogue

Women still made him nervous. And pregnant women? Yeah, they terrified him. Thankfully, Sienna had taken to motherhood like a champ. Blaine loved being with her. Every day. And that's why he was ready to take the plunge and ask her to marry him.

Every morning, he stopped by at 5:00 a.m. to feed the baby, and every morning when he held Madeline in his arms, he wanted her and Sienna to be officially his, so he could be with them all the time. A month old already, the baby was the cutest thing he'd ever seen. She had Sienna's eyes. He loved those green eyes.

Her ex, Troy, had been granted a fast track to successfully waive his parental rights. Sienna had found out last week, and she'd made her peace with it. Blaine planned on officially adopting Madeline as soon as they were married. She just had to say yes.

He opened the oven a crack. Yep. He was ready.

Flowers on the table. Lasagna and garlic bread in the oven. His dad had made the lasagna earlier and told him to bake it for forty-five minutes. Dad was a phenomenal cook, so Blaine wasn't worried about the meal.

He patted his pocket. Box was there. Ring was secured. He was good to go.

His heartbeat was pounding as he exhaled.

Last Friday, Blaine had made the mistake of telling the guys he was asking Sienna to marry him tonight. They'd thrown out the dumbest ideas he'd ever heard.

Sawyer said he should bake the ring into a puppy treat since she'd helped with the puppies. Blaine had hung his head in disgust. And Randy had, once again, thrown out the old fishing-rod-and-lure idea, although as a fisherman himself, Randy hadn't even used it on Hannah. Mac was no better. He'd suggested, "You should have Bridget put it in one of those frozen coffees Sienna likes so much."

To which Blaine had replied, "What if she chokes on it?" That had shut him up.

And Jet—his own brother—had told him to just let Mom and Reagan plan it. Uh, no.

So here he was, shaking like a leaf, waiting for her to arrive.

He'd ask her in his own way.

At the sound of her knock, he straightened his shoulders and went to the front door with Tiara and Ollie trailing behind him.

She had on a long, flowy shirt and black pants. Her hair waved around her shoulders. He pulled her inside and kissed her thoroughly.

"It was so sweet of your mom to watch the baby. She insisted we needed a proper date. But I told her we eat supper together every night, anyhow." She kept her arms around his waist. He could stay like this forever.

"My mom's always right. Don't try to fight it."

She laughed. "I won't."

He kissed her again.

"I feel like I've been in another universe lately. Feed the baby, change the baby, wipe the spit-up off my shirt, feed the baby again. It's a nice change to feel normal even if it's only for an hour." She lavished attention on both dogs before straightening.

"You're doing a great job. I don't know how you do it every day." He took her hand and led her down the hallway to the kitchen table, where he'd set two place settings, lit a candle and placed two dozen pink roses. "Those are for you."

"Oh!" She placed her hand over her heart. "This is so romantic."

"It should be. You deserve a little romance." He held the chair out for her to sit, and once she did, he closed his eyes and said a silent prayer. *Lord, give me the right words to let her know how much I love her.*

"The more I spend time with you and the baby, the more I want the three of us living in the same house. It's no secret I love you. And I want to share it all—the feedings, the spit-up, the everyday moments that make up a life. I know you need a cat, and we'll get a kitten whenever you want." He took out the jewelry box and got down on one knee, then he opened the box. "Sienna, will you marry me?"

"Yes, Blaine, of course, I'll marry you." Tears glistened in her eyes as she allowed him to slide the diamond ring on her finger. "How could I not if you're willing to share spit-up and get me a kitten? It has to be fluffy."

"Done." He chuckled, then kissed her.

"Do you want a big wedding like Randy and Hannah's?" Her eyebrows drew together slightly.

"I want whatever you want."

"So a smallish affair?"

"The smaller, the better." He grinned. "All I care about is that you say 'I do.'"

"I do."

"Then that's all I'll ever need. You're everything to me."

"Oh, Blaine…"

He kissed her again. She was his. He couldn't be happier.

* * * * *

*If you enjoyed this Wyoming Ranchers story
by Jill Kemerer, be sure to pick up the
previous books in the series:*

The Prodigal's Holiday Hope
A Cowboy to Rely On
Guarding His Secret
The Mistletoe Favor

Available now from Love Inspired!

Dear Reader,

Trauma can come in many forms. Both Blaine and Sienna had lost brothers. Blaine still struggled with the pain of being rejected by Cody before he died. And Sienna couldn't see that she was putting her own happiness aside because she feared losing her sister. Both Blaine and Sienna have such big hearts and I love how they bring out the best in each other.

That's how love is supposed to be. Unselfish and kind. With God's help, they were able to move beyond their pasts to hope for a better future together.

It's amazing what good friends, summer sunshine, puppies and prayer can do for a person. Oh, that we all could spend some time on a ranch in Wyoming with good friends, sunshine and prayer. And puppies, of course!

I hope you enjoyed this story. I love connecting with readers. Feel free to email me at jill@jillkemerer.com or write me at P.O. Box 2802, Whitehouse, Ohio, 43571.

Wishing you every blessing,
Jill Kemerer

COMING NEXT MONTH FROM
Love Inspired

FALLING FOR THE AMISH BAD BOY
Seven Amish Sisters • by Emma Miller

Beth Koffman is furious that Jack Lehman broke her sister's heart. But when her family hires him to build their store, she's the one elected to oversee the construction. As she gets to know him, she discovers there is more to Jack than meets the eye. Could he be her perfect match?

THE WIDOW'S HIDDEN PAST
by Rebecca Kertz

While visiting her sister in a neighboring town, widow Alta Hershberger meets handsome preacher Jonas Miller. Though she's not looking for love, she can't help her attraction to him. And he seems to feel the same. But how can they be together when she's running from her secret past?

A STEADFAST COMPANION
K-9 Companions • by Myra Johnson

Angus "Witt" Wittenbauer lost everything—even his beloved dog. Now he needs a safe place to land, and dog rescue center owner Maddie McNeill could be the answer. With a spring storm threatening, Maddie needs Witt to fix a leaky kennel roof. Can they also mend their broken hearts?

HIS ALASKAN REDEMPTION
Home to Hearts Bay • by Heidi McCahan

Crab fisherman Gus Colman is just trying to make a living. But when he's injured and stranded in Hearts Bay, he comes face-to-face with Mia Madden—his late best friend's fiancée. He works hard to prove he's changed, but can Mia ever love another man who risks his life at sea?

THE BRONC RIDER'S TWINS
Shepherd's Creek • by Danica Favorite

Convinced he caused his best friend's death, rodeo cowboy Wyatt Nelson wants to look after widow Laura Fisher and her infant twins. And a marriage of convenience is the perfect solution. But as Wyatt begins to fall for the little family, will he let guilt get in the way of his heart?

WINNING HIS TRUST
by Toni Shiloh

Back home after a breakup, Jordan Wood is determined to prove she can manage her family's general store. When single dad Declan Porter offers her a business opportunity, she jumps at the chance. Then she gets to know Declan's adorable son, and suddenly their professional relationship turns personal...

LICNM0123

Get 4 FREE REWARDS!

We'll send you 2 FREE Books plus 2 FREE Mystery Gifts.

FREE
Value Over
$20

Both the **Love Inspired®** and **Love Inspired®** Suspense series feature compelling novels filled with inspirational romance, faith, forgiveness and hope.

YES! Please send me 2 FREE novels from the Love Inspired or Love Inspired Suspense series and my 2 FREE gifts (gifts are worth about $10 retail). After receiving them, if I don't wish to receive any more books, I can return the shipping statement marked "cancel." If I don't cancel, I will receive 6 brand-new Love Inspired Larger-Print books or Love Inspired Suspense Larger-Print books every month and be billed just $6.49 each in the U.S. or $6.74 each in Canada. That is a savings of at least 16% off the cover price. It's quite a bargain! Shipping and handling is just 50¢ per book in the U.S. and $1.25 per book in Canada.* I understand that accepting the 2 free books and gifts places me under no obligation to buy anything. I can always return a shipment and cancel at any time by calling the number below. The free books and gifts are mine to keep no matter what I decide.

Choose one: ☐ **Love Inspired**   ☐ **Love Inspired Suspense**
                  Larger-Print   **Larger-Print**
                  (122/322 IDN GRHK)   (107/307 IDN GRHK)

Name (please print)

Address   Apt. #

City   State/Province   Zip/Postal Code

Email: Please check this box ☐ if you would like to receive newsletters and promotional emails from Harlequin Enterprises ULC and its affiliates. You can unsubscribe anytime.

Mail to the **Harlequin Reader Service:**
IN U.S.A.: P.O. Box 1341, Buffalo, NY 14240-8531
IN CANADA: P.O. Box 603, Fort Erie, Ontario L2A 5X3

Want to try 2 free books from another series? Call 1-800-873-8635 or visit www.ReaderService.com.

---

*Terms and prices subject to change without notice. Prices do not include sales taxes, which will be charged (if applicable) based on your state or country of residence. Canadian residents will be charged applicable taxes. Offer not valid in Quebec. This offer is limited to one order per household. Books received may not be as shown. Not valid for current subscribers to the Love Inspired or Love Inspired Suspense series. All orders subject to approval. Credit or debit balances in a customer's account(s) may be offset by any other outstanding balance owed by or to the customer. Please allow 4 to 6 weeks for delivery. Offer available while quantities last.

Your Privacy—Your information is being collected by Harlequin Enterprises ULC, operating as Harlequin Reader Service. For a complete summary of the information we collect, how we use this information and to whom it is disclosed, please visit our privacy notice located at corporate.harlequin.com/privacy-notice. From time to time we may also exchange your personal information with reputable third parties. If you wish to opt out of this sharing of your personal information, please visit readerservice.com/consumerschoice or call 1-800-873-8635. **Notice to California Residents**—Under California law, you have specific rights to control and access your data. For more information on these rights and how to exercise them, visit corporate.harlequin.com/california-privacy.

LIRLIS22R3

HARLEQUIN
PLUS

Try the best multimedia
subscription service for romance
readers like you!

Read, Watch and Play.

Experience the easiest way to get
the romance content you crave.

Start your **FREE TRIAL** at
<u>www.harlequinplus.com/freetrial</u>.